It All was a Lie!

A Brutal Encounter with Reality

Dr. Carlos Maldonado Ortiz

To my Son:
Tiny little gear of the perennial cycle.
Fleeting glint that unmasks the absurd,
that unravels death.

Ordering Information:

For orders and inquiries, please contact:
1-888-404-1388
www.goldtouchpress.com
book.orders@goldtouchpress.com

Printed in the United States of America

CONTENTS

CHAPTER I

SHIT IS SHIT IS SHIT

In Search of the Absolute

Along with his messy mop of hair they sent him to fuck his mother. And however much he tried to dissuade them; they all played the asshole. He spent the rest of his life insisting that the laws he had enunciated were only applicable to part of the physical world; not to the spiritual one and even less to morals. But they were very convenient for a world of mediocre and pusillanimous people, and he himself was taken as a symbol, wielding his ideas to justify the imbecility of the herd and its total loss of values and common sense. Thus, without having the slightest clue what he was talking about, they clung on to his concepts, and pretended that everything was relative; that the world was as each person wanted to see it, through their own lens; and as a logic and foreseeable consequence, ignorance plunged everything into chaos. Except that they forgot a very minute detail: *REALITY.*

And it's this "little oversight" what crumbles all illusions and perspectives, straight or warped; it is, this, the root of our misfortunes and sorrows. Because of it, the whole of traumas and frustrations that have disturbed mankind since time immemorial were born, giving rise in turn, to a frightful string of remedies and therapies, myths and legends, which have fed generations of sorcerers, healers, psychologists and other similar critters, **to** whom the bunch of assholes assumes to be less asshole than all the bunch of assholes. The problem is that, even if we want to close our eyes or flee from it, reality is always there, uncompassionate and inescapable, brutal.

To further complicate matters, sordid political interests coupled with the unbounded avarice of unscrupulous merchants, take advantage of the chaotic situation to attain their most aberrant objectives. Making use of an increasingly sophisticated marketing, they have managed to condition our behavior so much so that they make us consume even the unthinkable. With the mind and the sensibility obfuscated, we fell into the trap of the cult of fantasy worlds, where reality doesn't matter and the truth becomes unrecognizable. We thus have Prince Charmings, flying karatekas, friendly multicolored monsters and even pigs that speak; no offense intended, of course. They have convinced us that becoming absorbed in fiction promotes the intellectual development of the individual, even conjecturing that this is what has driven "the great creativity" that characterizes our pompous modern civilization. Nothing could be further from the truth. Overvaluing such mirages has impaired our perceptive ability. Deep in addiction to an artificial world, we want to destroy the true world, so that it does not disturb our delusion. Irrefutable proof is the stultifying propensity we have developed for videogames and cell phones. And it's worth noting the popularity of "cutting edge" software that allows us to have a fabulous "second life" where we can fulfill all of our desires. We want to live in a soap opera, artificially complicating things to put a bit of excitement in our routine existence, but without confronting real challenges and responsibilities. Faced with so many improvised values, without any foundation, an essential question arises: Does the absolute exist? Something that serves as a benchmark to evaluate everything else. And if it exists, can we put it aside without consequences? Here is a question that takes an entire life to answer, and that the vast majority try to avoid. Such are the enormous implications it entails.

When photography was newly invented, back then it was in black and white, even though some may not believe it, it had an unthinkable consequence: Light had to be rediscovered; to hone our understanding of its behavior and its capture by the human eye. As a parameter to measure the different luminosity of the tones that formed the images, the need arose to create a "Grayscale", whose ends were pure black and pure white. In the middle was a gradation of grays that emerged from the combination of both in different proportions. Black and white were the absolute, essential and immutable values that defined all the rest, and clarified our visual perception of the world. And nothing changed when colors appeared. For those paladins of tolerance whom the existence of solidly founded extremisms terrifies, bad news, no matter how much they want to Satanize them, reality is that black and white not only exist, but have a primordial and conclusive signification, they are indispensable components of Cosmos, darkness and light. The absolute is ineluctable. And it's not that we intend to see life in black and white, there are, simply, positive factors that liberate the individual, that give him spiritual peace and allow his intellectual development; and there are negative factors that sink him into slavery, that nullify him as a Human Being and condemn him to a life of uneasiness and frustration.

To find the elusive answer, sound judgment advises us to use the scientific method, whose foundation is the meticulous observation of the reality of Nature; which is just the group of beings, energy forces and matter forming the Universe in its primary state. No other possibility exists. Based on this scrutiny, theories are formulated, which must be demonstrable and repeatable with experimentation, and unarguable conclusions are drawn. So, let's analyze the environment that wrap us, with a critical spirit and a receptive mind, searching in it for transcendental, immutable values that can really serve us as a guide and clarify what we're here for. Incredibly, they are very simple and in plain sight for all to see. It immediately becomes clear that it suffices to observe reality to understand how we are integrated into the Universe. It's not a matter of creating ideological currents or believing absurd things; there is nothing to philosophize or redefine; in Nature everything is already determined. All the answers we seek are there. The first great truth that arises because of its overwhelming solidity and unquestionable importance is: Nature can live without man; but man cannot survive without Nature. A basic reasoning follows from this fundamental fact: We have the inescapable obligation to protect the well-being of Nature since it's indispensable for the well-being of man himself. Nature is not at our service. Therefore, *the survival of Nature takes* **priority** *over the survival of the Human Being.* There is no way to highlight more emphatically this **First Absolute Value**.

The most pressing challenge for today's civilization is the overpopulation of the planet. No matter how much scientists, theologians, politicians and many other outlandish creepy-crawlies get riled up, giving a solution to this clear and simple issue will solve, practically, all the problems that burden us: Insufficient food production; destruction and pollution of ecosystems to provide services, transportation and communication to a population in disproportionate growth; create sources of work, schools, hospitals for the new generations; and a very long etcetera. The origin of all is that the natural mechanisms of population control have been eliminated. And the main culprit for this catastrophe is medicine. From the initial laudable intention, they moved on to the perverse political and religious ideology of considering man's life as sacred, untouchable; we already even want to be immortal. To this has been added the morbid conception of health as a business; and the more customers the more money. And they have many "humanistic" arguments to adduce to protect their interests. Ironically, we're reaching the point where the life of a tree will be far more valuable than the life of a man.

I recall a study made in India by biologists who sought to save the Bengal tiger from extinction. The conclusion: A single tiger needed roughly fifty square kilometers of territory to satisfy its vital needs, and to be able, at the same time, to interact with its peers. The rest was a matter of doing a simple calculation to deduce how many felines fit in the available area and limit their number to attain their finest development. Logically, priority had to be given to the best specimens to maximize the possibilities of survival. Over time, numerous similar studies of various species have been conducted that give us a clear idea of the general panorama of the interaction among the beings that inhabit the earth. Inconceivably, there is not a single study that evaluates the prospects the man faces. How many individuals can fit in a place according to the natural resources available? How big must cities be so that people don't lose their human quality? How to reduce the waste that poisons our environment? Just as Physics and Chemistry have augmented our knowledge of the material world, the Sciences of Man should already have dictated at least the foundations of a pattern of human behavior. Nonetheless, after centuries of study, we have lacked the courage to overcome complexes and prejudices, taking refuge in the pretentious pretext of the "inextricable intellectual complexity" of man. It's not true that it's so complicated! The main obstacle is the current, artificial and grotesque hyper humanism. We like to feel special, unique; in our myopic conception we argue that it's not possible to judge man like any other animal. Reality, on the contrary, does not admit exceptions. It's stupid to claim that humanity has the right to occupy all space; to destroy the ecological balance, essential to sustain life on the planet. There is not a single government plan in the world that considers population control, on a natural basis, to maintain the well-being of its citizens. Programs conceived with political purposes have been a complete disaster. Judging by the propaganda they do; the rulers seem to have the intention of filling the entire surface of the earth with houses. By decree, they want to change the natural laws at their convenience. The truth is as simple as understanding that you cannot put ten tomatoes in a bag that can only hold five, without one another being ripped apart. We have the option of using intelligence to control the absurd population growth, or we can let Nature act to solve the problem, and accept the consequences of our own stupidity; simply, there no longer fit that much people. *The earth has a limited capacity!* Here is the **Second Absolute Value.**

They've talked to us so much about eternal life, about our heavenly kinship, that we ended up believing the tale of the "Children of God". Again, fantasy prevents us from evaluating the fragility and fleetingness of existence. Our inability to enjoy life is terrifying. Between fallacies and fabulous inventions, we spend hours looking for ways to "kill time" because we don't know how to take advantage of it. Technology has become our executioner. Stuck in unrestrained consumerism; they have convinced us that we're here to accumulate objects. We've forgotten the pleasure of doing creative and productive activities for fun. We're just passing through this world and our stay is very brief, there is no time to lose. It's not true that we are eternal! And about resurrection… We better not even talk; for not swearing at moms. *Life is a unique and fleeting experience.* This is the **Third Absolute Value.**

In Nature everything has a well-established order. In order to be able to reach more advanced stages, it's indispensable to meet certain requirements. A frog, before a frog, must be a tadpole, and have survived. As obvious as analyzing that only a surgeon, after preparing for years to acquire the necessary knowledge, is authorized to perform surgery. Or that only a well experienced engineer knows how to build a skyscraper. It's inadmissible for an ignorant person to want to have the right to express an opinion on matters of which he doesn't have the least element of judgement. Not all opinions are valid, much less respectable. For centuries people had the idea that the earth was flat and the center of the Universe. And not because millions of dumbasses believed that that bullshit was correct, it stopped being bullshit. You cannot and must not respect stupidity. Knowledge broadens judgment and provides grounds for being able to make an informed decision, but above all a valid one. If you want your opinion to be respected, you must begin by respecting yourself, getting prepared to be able to express yourself. We've forgotten the wise proverb: "Do not opine on what you don't know".

On the other hand, with commercial advertising besieging them mercilessly, the new generations have been persuaded that they are the most important thing and that they deserve everything. They are trapped in the immediate reward mentality. To be considered a celebrity for achievements without merit, and without making efforts or commitments. This is shamefully reflected in their adoration for sportspeople or so-called artists; a bunch of ignorant individuals without authentic qualities that advertising has transformed into heroes of a consumerist society, and they earn exorbitant salaries because they are very saleable products; even if they're just trifles. In contrast, teachers who have the invaluable task of preparing future generations, peasants who produce the foodstuffs that nourish us, or healthcare professionals who, after years of study, provide essential services, receive degrading wages. The great wishes of today are to be a football player or a "songster" to earn lots of money and be famous. That's how deformed our scale of values is; that's how serious domestication is. To reach maturity, wisdom, one must first gain experience by facing and adapting to reality; this costs discipline, dedication and perseverance. Rights are not given gratuitously. Nature irrefutably proves it: First you have to sow, water, care, for then be able to harvest, and that takes time and effort. *Rights are not demanded, they are earned by hard work, after fulfilling obligations.* Here we have the **Fourth Absolute Value.**

A sage adage goes: "He who was born to be a flowerpot, will always be in the hall". Nonetheless, with the tale of human rights, today it's claimed that we all have the right to everything, and that it's legitimate to demand such equity. Thus, we find many young people who, no matter what, want to study a university degree for which they don't have the necessary faculties, even though later they'll be mediocre professionals who are only going to cause damage to society. Whereas in ancient times, such as the Renaissance, excellence was the ultimate aspiration, nowadays we have lowered the standards to accommodate our negligence and laziness. The slogan is: Do not demand anything from me and I don't demand anything from you, let's enjoy our mediocrity. However, we feel deserving of accolades and distinctions. Any asshole thinks he's capable of creating, of innovating, of being a genius. We want to deny reality, but if talent is not brought in innately, simply, no fruits will be borne. Our genetic makeup specifies our physical, mental and spiritual capacities, which enables us to perform certain functions that will define the role that each person has to play, whether we like it or not. *We are not all equal!* Here is the polemical, but unquestionable, **Fifth Absolute Value**.

Given the brevity of human life, it's imperative to situate ourselves as soon as possible in time and space. But I'm not referring to a myopic vision of limiting ourselves to our country and time, but to becoming aware of our place in history and in the Universe. To slow down in order to be able to reflect, and perceive our surroundings. In the acceleration that characterizes this cybernetic age, in which we don't want to lose a second of connection in the "social networks" but we squander our lives in banalities, we have pretended that everything is valid, that each one can interpret things however they want and do whatever they want, no matter how grotesque it may be; in fact, the more grotesque the better, because, like this, morbidness is more exploited and it can even turn us into a "celebrity". We have forgotten the **Sixth Absolute Value**: *It is primordial to accurately define the fundamental concepts to clarify the ideas.* To know exactly what we're talking about! Otherwise, we're going to be shipwrecked in a sea of ambiguous notions, or worse yet, distorted or false, that divert us from the true meaning of things. The most serious thing is that this immoderate relativism has sunk us into a terrible confusion; we've fallen into an abyss of errors that lead us to waste life, instead of enjoying it. This takes us, lastly, to the **Seventh Absolute Value**: *Our deeds bring consequences.* What we do or stop doing not solely affects our only life, but transcends to the lives of others. We are in debt to a society that, badly or well, supplies our needs; and whether we want it or not we depend on it. If you wish to have total individual freedom to do whatever you feel like, you'll have to do the same as the indigenous peoples who live in isolated places, without technology; producing their food, building their houses and making their clothes themselves. If you do, you can be absolutely certain that this is going to radically change your conception of things. The point is that, just because of the simple fact of having to define it, even freedom has rules. We cannot restrict ourselves to the selfish approach that, whether what we do is good or bad is just our own business. This is not about moralistic or ethical questions. Our behavior imprisons us or liberates us, but also, like the aqueous waves that the drop creates when it falls into a pond, it spreads around us its light or its shadows.

In our great "liberating revolution" we want to put aside the natural laws and unleash our extravagances. The domestication of the individual has been so extreme and terrible that, in this maelstrom of ludicrous rights, we have even gone so far as to abolish our most elementary instincts. Thus, they can convince us that it's valid to eat excrement, although, as a residue of a natural physiological process, it's something repulsive that our body has discarded as unusable or toxic. Only a pig regards feces as a delicious delicacy. Reality admits no ambiguities. No matter how much we want to play the dumbass, *in the true world shit is shit is shit. And the more you stir it, the more it stinks.*

CHAPTER II

AND IN THE END, IT ALL WAS PURE WORDS

GOD?... OOOH MY GOD!

How could I have imagined it? If, even looking at it, feeling it, it was inconceivable, indecipherable. What a devastating immensity! What disquietude in the soul! So much loneliness in a simple corner; so many enigmas wandering through that unfathomable abyss. Isolated from civilization, immersed in the ravishing presence of the nocturnal landscape, under the star-studded sky, reality emerged brutally: How tiny and insignificant we are! How magnificent is the Cosmos! How many conflicting emotions beset the spirit, overpowering thinking, terrifying our Being! And all of a sudden, like a lightning breaking the darkness, the answer; the long-awaited answer, a thousand times implored: Thus, was born God! This is God! It was here where the human mind created a refuge against the overwhelming emptiness, uneasiness, helplessness;

a warm coat to wrap up, and escape fear, madness… nothingness. And it named it God.

Only those who have had the privilege of experiencing total communion with Nature; by going deep into it, accepting the challenge of being responsible for their own life; of facing atavistic fears, and defying the risks of finding their own path; they have had the opportunity to truly realize our smallness before the Universe. It's here when the consciousness of what led the Human Being to conceive the idea of God arises. After all, if man were the aim, all would be lost; dreams and wondrous things condemned to oblivion; nothing would remain to inspire us, to overflow us with fascination. In our insignificance, our brief passage on earth would be a waste. With our human potential dormant, we would never surpass the animal level. That was why man had the need to create God, and not the other way around.

Difficulties began when they tried to reinterpret reality. And from there an incredible variety of religions arose to satisfy all likings and requests, fostered by individuals who, without any consideration, saw in them the opportunity to satiate their thirst for power, controlling the others. In the beginning these beliefs were animistic, based on natural elements, imagining fantastic or "animaloid" beings, rooted in reality. These gods were cruel and demanding, requiring tribute and respect, which helped preserve Nature. When consciousness evolved, demigods and gods with human characteristics appeared. There we have the Greek mythology, copied and augmented by the Romans, in which the prelude to our accession to the throne is already glimpsed. The situation worsened with the advent of monotheism, the biggest calamity to ever have ravaged humankind. Thus, they came to conceive the poignant story of an unfortunate naïve guy who stupidly let himself to be martyred, wanting to redeem the irredeemable. Here it's key to highlight that religiosity needs physical objects to reinforce itself. That's why stone idols, icons of saints, relics and, finally, figures of truly humanoid gods appeared, as a reflection of our sick desires. As religious practices became more and more abstract, as in Protestantism, which eliminated religious images and, ultimately, the Church itself as a celestial intermediary, man ended up occupying the place of god. And having been made in his image and likeness, as a logical consequence he was given a predominant place on earth, becoming the King of Creation. In recent times, science and technology have contributed to expanding the "power" of man, consolidating him as god. With the capability to do whatever he covets, he has earned the right to dominate or destroy the planet and, why not? the entire Universe.

Judging by archaeological finds, we have over fourteen thousand years believing in god, and it has been of no use to our evolution. Namely, since the beginning of time, god's mission has been to bring order out of chaos, nevertheless, the belief in him has only created a more chaotic situation, which has worsened coexistence among individuals. One of the basic problems is that religion is inexorably dogmatic, that is, you have to believe in a series of bullshit and absurd things for it to be valid, if not, the whole belief falls apart catastrophically. So we have, for instance, a woman who, in ancient times, without artificial fertilization, gave birth to a child without being screwed, because having sexual intercourse was a sin! Already, from there, we began with a very flimsy, false basis. The other big problem lies in that the idea of god, in itself, is vulgar. Suffice it to put it on a human scale to give us a clearer idea. It's assumed that, after putting in order the universal disorder, among the functions of god should be those of bringing prosperity to the world, of dispensing justice by punishing evildoers, of helping the destitute, who, in principle, shouldn't even exist. But of all of them he doesn't do a single one. And if he's not solving people's problems, it's then worth wondering: What does god dedicate himself to? Once the Universe is finished, what work does he do in his day to day? For he must serve a purpose! What is he doing at this moment when hospitals are full of dying patients imploring his help, and do not receive the slightest consolation? Let's compare him to a father, because that is what god is said to be, who irresponsibly brings into the world a bunch of children, but doesn't take charge of their feeding, clothing or education; that, although he has all his time free, he spends it idling while his offspring make a mess and a half, however they please; that is, a totally irresponsible person. What do we call such a pig in our society? Immediately the situation reveals itself as a horrifying calamity. On the other hand, you just have to imagine a guy who wants everyone to revere him, and constantly thank him for his favors, that's how complex-ridden this poor stupid is, who, because he has the power, tries to fulfill all his whims, manipulating people's lives at his will. Who does not admit any complaint or questioning? Who wants total exclusivity; and that, furthermore, the sucker is eternal! Worse still, the great reward he offers is everlasting life by his side, as his damn flunky! Fuck! If we consider the possibility that God be real, the consequences are even more cataclysmic.

But, to base our beliefs beyond an irrational and vile animal feeling, as thinking human beings we have the inalienable obligation to interpret them with the intellect. Thus, in order to be consistent with the absolute principles already mentioned and to understand with precision what we're talking about, let us define, first of all, the proper and exclusive characteristics of a god; that is, what is it that makes God, God. This is of primary importance and derives from the most elementary logic, given the great relevance that this belief has for the people; otherwise, the idea degenerates into absurd fanaticism that borders on idiocy, and we run the risk of getting confused and ending up accepting a piece of crap as god. To begin with, God is NOT a form of intrinsic energy or an essence linked to the entire Universe, nor an unknown force, nor an amorphous concept, because in that case electromagnetism, electricity, ultrasound, the enigmatic force of gravity, the quantum world and even an aroma could be considered as divinities. The concept of god unavoidably implies the presence of a supreme, autonomous, self-aware being, dominating everything else, and possessing certain unique characteristics. The very *"holy books"* of various religions and some elaborate dissertations on them, painstakingly made by prominent theologians, establish them for us. Among the most basic and transcendental are the following: In the *first* place, a god is omnipotent, that is, he can do everything; there is nothing that can oppose his immense power, there is nothing he cannot accomplish. *Second,* God is omnipresent, which means that he is everywhere at the same time, that he's aware of everything that happens, nothing can be hidden from him. *Third*, he is omniscient, that is, he knows everything, past, present and what will occur in the future. There is nothing he ignores. And, *fourthly*, he is omnibenevolent, that is, his biggest concern is the well-being of his *Creation*, to deliver it from all evil. These are intrinsic attributes of him, which means that no one else can have them. A god who does not meet all of these requirements, who does not possess all of these primordial qualities, plainly and simply he is not God.

The secondary divine attributes, which, by the way, are called communicable, because, by divine intercession, they can be transferred to man, and which, together with the theological virtues should be, in theory, the aspiration of all religious of yesterday, today and always, are goodness and mercy, which in God are infinite. And here a frankly monstrous and risible situation arises, which shows us all the momentousness of the difficulties that our belief in a god entails. I remember a horrific occurrence of a little baby who was kidnapped. Besides of how outrageous the case was, being about a totally defenseless being, it was devastating to watch the mother crying on television, begging the kidnappers to give her back her little girl because she had no money to pay a ransom, no matter how small; the kidnappers had got the wrong victim. It is not hard to conceive the desperation, humility and fervor with which this mother pleaded with God to return her daughter safe and sound, to soften the hearts of the criminals. But neither all her devotion nor her supplications could move the omnibenevolence and infinite mercy of God. The little girl was found dead a few days later, they had asphyxiated her with a plastic bag and then burned the little body, throwing it in a vacant lot. The worst nightmare a parent can ever imagine, come true before the eyes and indifference of God. And this case is not the only one, similar incidents are counted in the millions. For centuries the most erudite theologians have fruitlessly wracked their brains trying to justify the unjustifiable; to find an explanation for why God plays the dumbass in the face of so much barbarism. After pondering ad nauseam inadmissible reasonings, they give up faced with the undeniable facts, and always end up wielding the poor and nebulous argument that we cannot judge his actions because "God's hidden designs are incomprehensible". Aren't we supposed to be made in his image and likeness? It's an authentic madness to pretend that God, with all his magnificence, does not have the slightest concept of elementary logic, the minimal common sense. Behind this archaic pretext, this perverse veil of complicity, in the absence of legitimately valid conclusions, countless generations of malefactors, self-proclaimed heavenly messengers, have been hidden. Based on the supposed authority of grotesque and idiotic dogmas invented by themselves, they have manipulated the crowd to maintain their domains of power and justify massacres and atrocities. Religion as a weapon of subjugation and domestication, which appeals to the most basic instincts of man to consolidate its dominance.

We've already analyzed how the idea of a god arose from the need of the human soul to calm its unease, its terror and confusion faced with the overwhelming presence of an inexplicable, ungraspable Universe. This helped man in the early stages of his intellectual development to find the quietness and spiritual peace indispensable for his evolution, just as a walker assists a baby to learn to walk. Nevertheless, on maturing his intellect, and just as a baby-walker would be for a healthy adult, such a concept became a hindrance. Today it's not only obsolete but increasingly noxious. History bears witness to how many aberrations, cruelties and stupidities the notion of a deity has caused. It's been already a long time since the idea served its purpose, man learned to unravel his environment, to walk; just as we let the dead rest in peace, it's the moment to put it aside. In fact, even with the limited knowledge that has been acquired in the attempts to elucidate the universal structure, all indicates that there is no place in it where to put him. The Universe has no room for god! Just as the heaven inhabited by divine beings disappeared when science took us beyond the clouds, just as the earth ceased to be the center of the Universe and became round, the idea of god has been shattered by knowledge. But what is truly essential and transcendental is that god is not needed; it's irrational that that be the motive to be good and honest. And, after all, celestial power is not all it's cracked up to be. As grandparents said: "Not even God can take back words".

For hundreds, thousands of years, religious, politicians and even philosophers have speculated that man without god would be lost. The missionaries of the colonial era in America criticized the natives because by living as "savages" in Nature, without god or conscience, they lost control falling into "diabolic" behaviors, such as idolatry or polygamy, which led to their perdition. These are sheer bullshit! Actually, it's quite the opposite. Nature easily replaces god, and in spades. Unlike god, Nature is a tangible entity that awakens our senses; that we can see, touch, smell, hear, savor; and that, in addition to enthralling us and filling us with emotions, it's useful and quite predictable, so much so that we can entrust our lives to it. On being able to perceive its presence and feel ourselves a part of it, the fascination of sublime sensations and feelings enrapture us, giving an incommensurable depth and meaning to human existence, despite our insignificance. This is what the true Human Being has sought for time immemorial, the genuine explorer. Not like the alpinist full of hubris who intends to conquer the mountains and tries to demonstrate his supremacy, but the one who, getting rid of sordid desires for competition, makes the most of the invaluable opportunity to approach them with humility, to understand his own smallness, to learn to confront and overcome his fears, his complexes, his indolence. To engage with them in a liberating dialogue to integrate himself into the harmony of Nature. Nothing like the infinitude of space or the immensity of the sea to calm our uneasiness. Nothing like the quietude of the desert to find peace, or the fragrance of the forests and fields to inebriate our spirit.

But what is the kernel of all this fucking tale of communing with Nature? Why such a fuss? Simply because, on taking cognizance of the role he plays in Nature, the Human Being finds the satisfaction of his authentic ideals: The meaning of life, happiness and true liberty. Not the silly concept that we have in our civilization, where we arrive at the absurdity of considering ourselves free because we buy in one store rather than in another, or because we consume one product instead of another. We're talking about the liberty that allows the soul to expand, the mind to create its own ideas. Not being carried away by dogmatism, by advertising, by fashions; not getting caught up in the quest for God, for Paradise. Religion was conceived to control the pusillanimous ones, who use it to justify their servility, their slackness, their cowardice, and who find in it someone who forgives all these to them and gives them comfort. God as a justification for imbecility and a parapet for mediocrity. What are we going to do without god? Just hold the reins of our own existence. Have the courage to make decisions, fulfill our responsibilities and accept the consequences of our actions and mistakes. God and religion threaten the freedom of the individual. The point is that true liberty brings about a multitude of obligations that we don't want to deal with for the simple reason that they pit you against yourself, the worst possible enemy. This, of course, terrifies the mediocre, who need to leave their destiny in the hands of someone else, go with the flow, putting the blame onto others and hope that a higher being will magically solve their problems. The classic justification for submissively accepting a miserable life because dear god has not wanted to help us out of it. We don't want to pay the price, which includes discipline, temperance, perseverance, fortitude, commitment. The philosophers of yesteryear already intuited it: *"Man must be compelled to be free"*.

Another argument employed to support the belief in god is that man has a natural need to know the origin of things, and logically having an answer about the creation of the Universe would be crucial. But, on the one hand, given its immeasurable magnitude and its remoteness in time, it's a question to which we're never going to be able to give a precise response, and it has only lent itself to boastfulness and harebrained assumptions, to the taste and measure of each one. In any case, what REAL importance would it have to know the answer? This is as stupidly irrational as claiming that in order to be able to live our adult life it's essential to know what happened in the days of our embryonic stage, when our consciousness was not even born yet. What is relevant is that we're already here and human life is too short to waste making ludicrous conjectures. This does not contradict the wisdom of the saying: "The peoples who forget their history are condemned to repeat it". Quite simply, we have to deal with the real human problems that we can actually solve, by drawing lessons from the past; by studying the social practices and achievements of antiquity, documented or verifiable, in order to take advantage of what may be helpful to us. What good is it for us to know how the earth was formed if we have not even learned to take care of it, not to destroy it? On the other hand, it's a lie that man has an innate need to know the origin of things, that's a quality limited to a few perspicacious spirits. If you do not believe it, just try to answer: How does a cell phone, an automobile or a refrigerator work? When have you lost sleep over not knowing it? Or simply, when have you ever wondered who made your television, your shoes or the clothes you wear? Is it because maybe we have a presentiment that it's the product of slave labor, and it's better to play the fool to continue living our dream of modernity? The mediocre and pusillanimous ones do not give a damn about the origin of things. They're only interested in the I in the here and now; the dining, crapping and screwing; safety, even if they have to be tied to a yoke.

One of the most serious consequences to which the notion of god has led us is that we've fallen into a deformed, pretentious and hypocritical hyper humanism, beyond the human, which has finally led us to dehumanization. We insist on considering instinctive attitudes such as aversion or ire as detrimental, which are natural attributes with which man has been endowed, and which have been crucial for his defense and preservation in an aggressive and demanding world. Adamant about emphasizing our "superiority" over the other animals, rejecting and despising their supposed "wild" behaviors, we ended up becoming worse beasts. We want to get rid of such conducts just to satisfy our twisted concepts of goodness and morals out of all reality, without rationally evaluating their function, and their indubitable usefulness. Nothing is more idiotic than the idea of lions and gazelles behaving like lambs, coexisting in peace, instead of "in harmony", the natural harmony of the Universe. Facing reality and realizing the falsehood of many preconceived dreams and goals that they conditioned us to believe, and that perhaps satisfied our most utopian ideals, do not have to disappoint us, to depress us, or to make us lose the joy of living; on the contrary, truth sets us free and puts things in their place to know what to expect, and how to prepare to defend ourselves. We're not the navel of the world and man is not as special as they want to make us believe. Despite this, life is a wonderful adventure and the motivations to live it are inexhaustible. But the first requisites to reach maturity, wisdom, and the happiness that they entail, are the acceptance of our limitations and the comprehension of the grandeur of the Universe in which we are immersed, and over which we have no control whatsoever.

And, taking a parenthesis, I'm going to take the liberty of doing an incendiary conjecture, which perhaps will bring us a bit of consolation by corroborating that the worries that overwhelm us today also lacerated the souls of our predecessors. I want to assume that, with so much advertising abuse that has been made of it, everyone knows the image of the Creation of Man painted by Michel Angelo on the vault of the Sistine Chapel. I remember that from the first time I saw it, up there in the heights, immediately caught my attention the great effort that a group of angels seems to be doing to transport God the Father. Not only did it seem funny to me but even insolent to insinuate that God was very heavy, so much so that a multitude was needed to carry him. It also seemed strange and inexplicable to me a sort of purple linen that serves as a background to the group of Gods with the angels, since it appeared to have no function; after all, it was the poor angels who were taking the beating. Years later, a dedicated scholar of the subject suggested that the shape of the linen represented a cerebral hemisphere viewed from a lateral perspective; he even identified the anatomical parts of it, which matched with astonishing precision. This painter being an accomplished anatomist, the probabilities that such a hypothesis be true are extremely high. But, a brain!? For what reason? And here I'm going to infer the diabolical idea that the image of god, which, very suspiciously, is entirely contained within the "brain", represents the notion that god is only in our imagination, inside our mind, that God does not exist! And that religion has been a burden that innumerable generations have had to carry on their shoulders, symbolized by the willful angels. Knowing the irreverent and critical temperament of Michel Angelo, coupled with the presence of more provocative images in the Sistine Chapel itself and in some other of his works, the fresco of Creation could be a veiled expression of his own stance, a surreptitious condemnation of the corrupt and perfidious behavior of the clergy of the time. Suffice it to consider the circumstances, it was the Renaissance and Luther's Reformation was in the making. Exalted by the light of a new awakening, it would be like embedding a blasphemy, a heresy, smack in the heart of the decrepit ecclesiastical empire. Quite an audacity. Not for nothing that guy was a genius indeed.

As a sole, enlightening and very elaborate explanation of the origin of Cosmos, for centuries and more centuries the Church has solemnly repeated to us the dogmatic phrase: "In the beginning was the Word". But over time truth has become evident: In the end it all was pure words; sheer fucking chatter. The foundations of our conduct must be based, uniquely, on the reality of Nature. The existence of God does not have to trap us in a ridiculous dilemma. To get involved in the sterile controversy of whether he is real or not, is an absurd waste of precious time, permissible only for unavailing people, prone to a futile life. The truly crucial question, the one that needs to be answered, is: What is god useful for? If his presence is not going to have a tangible usefulness for the Human Being, what do we want him for? A god who with all of his inexhaustible goodness is not going to ACTIVELY intervene to help us resolve the earthly problems, what role does he play then? God as an idea is lamentable; as an entity he's despicable. The conception of a divine being who, knowing everything in advance and having all the power to solve or avoid things, seems impassive and indolent in the face of war, kidnapping, murder and so many other perversities, is so repugnant and frightening that, for our own good, he had better not exist! And if god is real, well, better yet, in order to be able to blaspheme at ease. A good-for-nothing and bastard god must be sent to fuck his mother, even if he exists!

CHAPTER III

NEITHER FURTHER THITHER NOR NEARER HITHER

Of the Living and the Dead, just pure Tales!

All I want is a woman! He screamed in anguish, wide-eyed, on the brink of madness, as he jerked violently rubbing his penis with his warped hands to masturbate himself. It was a desperate, wrenching outcry. His mother, aghast and fed up, turned her face for not seeing him, and with a tone of justification she said to me in a muffled voice: *"Look at him, he's sick in the head"*. At his almost thirty years of age, the cerebral palsy that a complicated parturition left him only allowed him to clumsily move his misshapen hands and grotesquely utter almost unintelligible words. A pitifully lucid mind in an unusable body, tied to a wheelchair. And all I could do was sedate him; to help him escape this world; to which he didn't belong. The lady was already very old. In her alleged hyper human commiseration, and in order to exonerate herself of her terrible incapability to understand the meaning of life, and to satiate her enormous egoism, she didn't dare to let him die when he was a child, as Nature tried many times, and she condemned her only son to a life of inconceivable agony and suffering. But that was just the beginning, when she died and left him alone, helpless, turned into a wreck, the gates of hell were opened to the poor man, here on earth.

Terrifying stories like this have been constantly repeated in my professional life. The more "civilized" the communities are, the more we move away from the human sense of life, the more frequent they are. No profession like that of medicine to offer to an open mind and an inquisitive spirit the possibility of getting to know man; of witnessing his conduct before the most extreme situations of existence; of scrutinizing his comportment from its most sublime facets to its most bestial and aberrant behaviors. The big problem today is that we have confused humanism with prudery. Instead of offering the terminally ill patient a short term, dignified and compassionate natural death that quickly ends his suffering, we take advantage of the conjuncture to satisfy our morbid pretention of possessing an ultrahuman sensibility. It doesn't matter that we're just prolonging the pain, the agony, in a grotesque expression of cruelty, a mask of pseudo humanism that hides a wicked selfishness that refuses to resign itself to the loss of a loved one, not for the good of that person, but because of what his death implies for us. The excuse we use is sarcastic, a taunt: "It would be inhuman to let him die without doing anything for him". At the peak of our pedantry, we feel scandalized and condemn an act way more merciful: To let Nature act. If a person is not fit to lead a full life, where he can dream, enjoy and be free, why do we prolong his ordeal so perversely? If Nature has already determined that a being is not qualified for life, because he does not meet the most elementary requisites it has imposed, why do we insist on becoming gods and trying to make him survive, whatever it takes?

History provides us with a remarkable and instructive example of commiseration that shows us the way forward: Thousands of years ago, Greek civilization not only made flourish a society that reached excellence in artistic and intellectual expression, but also achieved a remarkable technical and scientific advance that revolutionized its era; besides of developing a system of laws and of community organization so evolved that it laid the foundations of a social structure that expanded throughout the Western world, and even nowadays it's a basic component of our own modern society. Nevertheless, being a culture linked to Nature, they instituted a selection system for its members that summarily eliminated babies born with physical deformities or mental disabilities; a custom that for our "advanced", ultrahuman moral values would be unacceptable. Despite this, at no time did this practice dehumanize them or lessen their sensibility and capability to attain an apogee as humanity has rarely achieved; that's how solid its principles and the guidelines on which it was based were. And we don't even need to go back in time. The same thing occurs in many indigenous groups that are still governed by natural laws. When a child is born with some disability or deformity, as soon as he falls ill, they let him die. For they are wicked and possessed by the devil? No, they're just trying to survive.

Very far back in the past remained the desires of the first medical researchers who only sought to reduce the suffering that overwhelmed humanity. With vaccines, surgery and anesthesia, analgesics and antibiotics, we had more than sufficient weapons to maintain a healthy and stable population. We succeeded in controlling and curing a good part of the diseases, pain was diminished and the standards of living were greatly improved, what made life duration to have a reasonable increase. The rest were innate problems that should have never been allowed to advance, not only because they are incurable, but because they impede a life of human quality. But this progress was spoiled when, in tune with our "progressive" ideology, medicine became a business. Vitiated interests that conceive health and illness as consumer products prevailed. The therapeutic ideal of "prevention rather than medication" has been pushed aside because it's not profitable. Sickness is an inexhaustible source of profit, even more so when the lucrative trade of death is added. Today the objectives of "medical science" have radically changed; our goals are superfluous and banal things: To look pretty, not to age, and, if possible, immortality. To this have been added the diseases that we ourselves have provoked with so much unnecessary and harmful technology. Although health traders are delighted, with the opening of innovative research fields, their fruitful market promises juicy dividends. In the past people died with dignity at home, surrounded by their loved ones. Today, isolated in ultramodern hospital units, under the care of strangers, we are negotiable merchandise, and a humiliating death is reserved for us, turned into human wreckage.

Health is the key element to keep the body functional, which is nothing more than a case to protect, harbor and transport the essential components of the human being: The mind and the soul. Health is the indispensable parameter with which Nature determines who deserves survival. Disease, whether of natural origin, from birth or by contagion, or through our own fault, as a reflection of our stupidity, is the mechanism to control population and allow only the best adapted individuals to survive. In Nature the useless is eliminated, mediocrity has no place in it. Hence the obligation we have to maintain our health, as it's one of the great gifts that is given to us, and not everyone is fortunate to receive it.

In the current debauchery of consumerism, excesses are the order of the day. One of the most serious problems affecting our society is being overweight. Never in history had existed so much useless lard. Obesity is a crime against humanity. And it's not that physical appearance be an affront to esthetics, even when the sight of a deformed and grotesque being instinctively gives rise to repugnance in us. Fatness is a serious health problem that wreaks havoc on society due to the economic deterioration that the treatment of its complications entails. That without considering the overload that the need to produce larger resources to feed them means for the planet. But the most crucial and scary point is that obesity is a reflection of the subculture of minimal effort, minimal commitment, the uncompromising pursuit of comfort. The mindset that we deserve it all, even if we have not done anything to earn it. Making eating a monstrous pleasure represents, tragically, a failed attempt to escape from the inner emptiness. What in Nature was intended for survival, we have turned into a vice.

And it's not the only one. Our decadent society is plagued with abuses and aberrant behaviors. Spiritual degradation has impaired interpersonal relationships and individual development; we're sunk in squandering, banality, ostentation. But there is no way of dodging reality, and even when advertising tries to convince us that we are super happy geniuses, and that there is nothing else we could wish for, the suffocating mediocrity that corrodes us inevitably becomes evident. When the hollowness of the mind and the extinct soul surface, life loses all meaning and the void that wraps us becomes, then, tangible. Neither money, nor luxuries, nor fame, nor savage materialism manage to satisfy us. Have you heard of the suicides of the superrich and famous who have it all? They truly have nothing. But, lo and behold, like a fantasy superhero, drugs come to the rescue; which have also opened the great opportunity of a lucrative business for the "visionary entrepreneurs" who know how to take advantage of the misfortune of others. Alcohol in the first place, which, despite being as harmful and despicable as any other drug, is considered "socially acceptable" by our hypocrisy, and the drug addicts who consume it can pass themselves off as respectable persons. The serious damages it inflicts not only to the individual but also to the community matters little. Do you have any idea how many injuries, mutilations and deaths are caused by inebriated drivers?

And from there into the abyss, using more and more potent and addictive drugs to alienate us till we become beasts, until we end up drooling through the streets. Sacks full of shit who pretend their weaknesses make them more human. Cowards who try to ignore their culpability in the dire conflicts that drug trafficking causes in the production sites, where rivalries and death destroy entire families. But we must escape whatever the cost. One of the justifications for using, say, marijuana, is that, being a plant, it's something natural that serves to liberate us, a blessing of Nature. This is a malicious and pernicious lie. In the first place, a healthy body possesses all the qualities that are needed to be happy and free, it does not require external stimulants. A balanced nutrition suffices to sharpen the senses, which are our sole natural means to be in contact with our environment and enjoy it. Fruits and vegetables, to speak of plants, have no point of comparison with hallucinogenic plants, which, in fact, are harmful to health, and even lethal. Second, the hallucinatory effect of the alkaloids is never liberating nor does it lead us to a transcendental astral journey, quite the opposite, it deranges and imprisons the mind in unreality, it limits perception by dulling the senses with mirages that sink us into a fictitious world, and it ends up stupefying the individual, by gradually undermining and destroying the brain. But that's exactly what the person is looking for, to escape from his dreadful reality, from the meaninglessness of a hollow life that he no longer has the courage to face. And we still have the gall to blame the physician who prescribes us opioids, in order to absolve ourselves of the responsibility for addictions that are a consequence of our pusillanimous character and our complacency towards a decrepit society.

And the list of noxious practices is endless, just as much as our degeneration and integration into a sick and superfluous civilization. It's not true that we must know and experience it all to understand life; there are harmful experiences that cause irreparable damages, and even drag us into criminal behavior. Distorted sexual practices, just like drugs, have become a palliative to cope with our captivity. Likewise, the fashion for piercings and tattoos feeds on slaves. What vainly pretended to be a symbol of autonomy and independence, like many other false liberating attitudes, became a mark of domestication and subjugation; and a blessed sweet deal for charlatans. Thus, we have a mediocre one who, given his lack of natural attributes, brands himself as cattle, flaunting his belonging to a herd, as the only way to stand out. A tattoo is a vile testimony of taming, of slavery, as yesteryear, which labels a weak mind that cannot create its own ideas. As long as modern society refuses to admit that it's a failed attempt and that the path must be rectified; as long as it's unable to refocus its values and give priority to a rapprochement with the natural world in order to find a true existential motivation, it will have to resort to drug addiction and self-destruction to escape a pusillanimous existence based on consumerism as a stupid goal of life. Essential causal factors have been the contempt and detachment from family that have caused its disintegration. Without the primordial pillar that supported it, it hopelessly flounders. With null and indolent men mating with vain women, supposedly well liberated but useless to forge a home, succeeding generations are condemned to a bleak future. What good is so much material wealth in the face of so much spiritual poverty? We fail to understand that human life only has meaning when it's useful, and, in the first place, useful to the universal cycle of existence. It's a natural law that we find everywhere; the sun not only provides us with the beauty of a sunset, it's at the same time fecund, giver of life. From this, it's deduced that serving is what will give us satisfaction and meaning to our presence on earth. It's essential to feed the soul, so that it does not die! Dreams are the natural mechanism for resting the brain and counteracting pressures. Drugs, to the contrary, provoke an overstimulation that exhausts the mind with so many hallucinations. If you need to evade yourself, go sleep, in order to dream. The least we must demand of someone is to take care of his own life, to take charge of his own health.

But it's not the first time this has happened. Whenever man departs from Nature to, supposedly, "progress" driven by his "irrepressible genius", he ends up plunging into the most depraved excesses that finally lead him to debacle. The King of Creation is inexorably trapped in an eternal cycle of imbecility. The explanation is very simple: Due to the oblivion of the past and our arrogance we have lost the perspective of the depth of time. Ignoramuses abound who think the world was created yesterday, that the past is obsolete and discardable for it's inapplicable in our "magnificent" modern civilization. A glimpse at history allows us to realize that everything is cyclical, that technological advance is inconsequential; be it arrows or rifles, the human being is the same and the experiential situations immutable. What we're living today has already been lived by countless previous generations, and we can learn a lot by analyzing how problems were handled or solved at the time, to improve our own response to them. It's idiotic to start from zero every time. A couple of clarifying examples: The unknown challenges we face with AIDS are cited as novelty, because before it didn't exist, or was not detected; but there were tuberculosis, syphilis or even typhoid fever, which back then were as deadly and unknown as AIDS is today. Our narrow perspective does not let us perceive that what is significant is man's reaction before death, which remains the same as it was millennia ago. And another even more eloquent: The challenge of the discovery of America was incomparable, and more relevant for humanity, than the moon landing itself. There is nothing new under the sun!

Any doctrine that wish to imply that we're the center of the Universe is an aberration. Although to the scale of our life it seems static, it's in a constant evolution, of which we're not witnesses. We're not the parameter to measure it. Our hubris obfuscates us, we've granted ourselves an importance we do not have in reality. We're not even a speck of dust. Our alleged progress, of which we feel so proud, is actually a regression, an ever-growing distancing from Nature that has made us lose many of the qualities we had. To insist on reaching a goal that has no subsequent usefulness is an absurdity, and yet that is the basis of consumerism! Not only do we live useless lives, but we've lost the notion of how to enjoy life and not become automatons. The point is that what we believe is insubstantial, we're not the ones who are going to define things, it's Nature that thousands of years ago ALREADY defined them. Totally opposed to the prevailing egocentric tendency, the more you forget of yourself, the more you try to make yourself useful to the society in which you live, the more the purpose of our ephemeral existence becomes evident. A question to finish off our insolent haughtiness: How would the Universe be affected if, in a horrendous cosmic cataclysm, our "sophisticated culture" perished; in which the ultimate expression of "progress" is to make the minimal effort possible. To be lying in front of a television eating snacks and getting high on alcohol; watching sports or a string of silly movies that are a true insult to the human intellect. Where is the big tragedy if a civilization of pigs like the present one becomes extinct!?

And speaking of the dead, let's stop for a moment to analyze an overly intriguing topic. Ever since the dawn of humanity, for countless generations in all cultures and civilizations of the planet, there have constantly been narratives and references to the perception of forces or enigmatic intangible beings that populate an unknown realm that surrounds us, and that, under certain circumstances, they irrupt into our world becoming perceptible, palpable, causing us great disquietude and dread. Phantoms, they called them, for lack of a better appellation, and with them arose the concepts of the errant soul of the dead and the afterlife. Nevertheless, science, its strict requirements not being met, takes a disdainful stance towards these accounts, branding them as superstitions. However, if we manage to overcome our arrogance and give ourselves a chance to investigate them with a receptive mind, we may find that they have a perfectly comprehensible and rational natural cause. It's as simple as picturing the reaction of a caveman if we put him in front of a television. In his ignorance and not having a logical explanation, he would imagine it to be some magical or diabolical vision, a witchcraft from out of this world; but we know that it's a simple electromagnetic wave receiver that reproduces images and sounds. It is exactly the same thing that happens to us with these energies capable of crossing walls, which we call "specters", whose provenance and way of acting we don't know. And the unknown scares us; even more so if for millennia we have accumulated absurd ideas that fill us with terror. Do you remember Anubis, Dracula, the Chupacabra? The most ridiculous thing is that after so many centuries of science we still have not had time to study and decipher these energy phenomena that have so much unsettled us, and we'd rather waste it on inventing weapons, devising techniques to domesticate our behavior or sending robots to other planets. But there is a promising new scientific field. The latest discoveries of the intricate quantum physics, with its inscrutable enigmas, hint at the possibility of the existence of a multidimensional space that would accommodate uncanny particles that seem to be in two places at the same time, or disappear and reappear spontaneously, as if defying our curiosity and perspicacity, as if reasoning! These odd findings could open a new path that leads us to unveil one of the most ancient mysteries the human being has faced. To discover new and unsuspected forms of energy that we have not even realized and that might hold the key to more momentous revelations. Let's refer to the past, when X rays or ultrasound were discovered, which pass through the body without us even being able to feel them, and they became indispensable tools for modern medicine. Nature is absolute; the supernatural, the paranormal does not exist, everything belongs to this universe, everything is subject to natural laws. The fact that we have not managed to unravel and comprehend the sidereal space in all its dimensions, that we don't know the origin of many things, does not make valid the invention of imbecilic fantasies and demons. The earth is round.

It is not necessary that there be a god or a heaven where we live for all of eternity by his side. We are already in a perennial universe, and we are already here forever! When we die, our molecules reintegrate into the universal cycle to keep on creating life; another form of life; they become part of another being, be it animal, vegetal or mineral; because rocks are also alive, they are born and die like us, but their rhythm of life is far slower, and their existence far longer, even though the brevity of ours does not allow us to perceive it. Lavoisier already said it more than two centuries ago: "Matter cannot be created nor destroyed; it simply changes form". When we manage to grasp this reality, we realize that, in essence, death does not exist! From this principle, which ancient man intuited without being able to specify it, the idea of reincarnation, of animism, was born. Even so, these transformations are what cause us pain, especially when we have not the least idea of what's happening, and even more so when it's about the decease of a person whom we have deeply loved; who had walked with us throughout our life. So, let's cry for them to mitigate the grief of their absence, to console our sadness. But let's understand that the dead stay forever with us, perhaps right by our side, in a tree or a flower, accompanying us. Let's scatter their remains throughout the world so that they keep on giving new life; so that they continue perpetuating the harmonious cycle of Cosmos. A natural cycle that goes far beyond god, an alternation of creation and destruction that constitutes the very essence of the Universe.

Death does not have to be something so dreadful, so unbearable, that we even come to desire it when we lose a loved one. It's essential to know its function and meaning to confront it, since it's a fundamental and unavoidable stage of the life cycle, life feeds on death. We must teach it to our children as an indispensable requisite for our evolution; learning to die is part of our integration into Nature. Even the Aztecs already had a clear notion of it. That's how frightful our regression is. In the end, it turns out that it's the most natural and common thing in the Universe. Even the stars die! It is risible to want to get into a bubble or be frozen to escape from it. The biggest problem to overcome is the perverse conception that has been forcibly instilled in us over the centuries, exacerbated by the religious concept of god and immortality. By pretending to ignore its existence we have been left emotionally unprotected. Our haughtiness and ignorance are the real inferno. The big irony is that, rather than a calamity or an enemy, death is our great and misunderstood ally, as its brutal arrival is a shock to our conceited egocentricity and arrogance. Feeling its presence brings us back to reality, makes us mature, humanizes us, and restores humility that we're so lacking nowadays. Coping with this absolute truth leads us to become aware and really value our fleeting passage on earth as humans; it alerts us that life is a unique opportunity, and woe betide those who don't know how to make the most of it! Just as life must be respected, death must also be respected. We're not gods nor are we immortal. There is a time to live and there is a time to die. Death is, simply, the impregnable bastion where life defends itself. There is no further thither; there is no nearer hither...

CHAPTER IV

YEAH, I BET SO!

The Abyss of Absurdity

Penises and vaginas; it seems it all is limited to that. If they repeat it so much, maybe it's true, don't ya think, Panchou? And it's that the "decommunication" media harp on about it with such tenacity, constantly, and displaying images of voluptuous little sluts posing sensually, showing their titties and their butt cheeks. Do they want, perhaps, to hammer the idea into our heads by force? What is true is that you get so befuddled that you end up imagining that at any moment the flying dick is going to appear crossing the skies; and that the objective of existence is limited to the life of the DCS (*decease*): Dining, Crapping, and Screwing; like pigs, like in the Lost Paradise that many still long for. Everything else has no value whatsoever.

The point is that we have given a sick importance to sex, totally out of its natural function. To untangle things let's do a simple mathematical exercise. Let's imagine that a super sexual being existed, like the one that commercial advertising incessantly brags about. The most fucking fucker of all fuckers that ever existed and that will ever exist; a bastard who needs to have coitus eight times a day. Now let's speculate that in each screw he spends half an hour, effectively, with the erect penis inserted inside the vagina, banging on and on. Next let's suppose he begins his sexual life at a very early age, let's say at twelve years old, since he must at least reach the age at which the hormonal system is usually activated; and he finishes it very late, let's say at eighty years old; as even for the most fucking fucker of all fuckers sexual drive also wanes, that is his dick dries up and it only serves to pee, and at times not even for that anymore. Finally let's imagine that our hypothetical super hero of screwing, let's call him Super Big Dick, *just to make a mess of it*, dies at ninety years of age. If we made a calculation supposing that all of human life lasted one single day, that is twenty-four hours, our amazing super hero would only spend three hours and two seconds fucking! Namely, a lot less time than he would spend sleeping, eating or even shitting, if he is often caught by "the runs", as my grandmother said. That's how important sex really is in our lives. Now, we're talking about our hypothetical hero Super Big Dick; but for a good part of normal mortals this time would be reduced to one tenth, that is, to about eighteen minutes, and for the vast majority, still a great lot more; and that's counting up masturbations! And the same is true for women, although in them the interest in procreation appears at an earlier age because the decline of sexual drive and the end of their fertile life occur earlier; this in spite of the uproar that feminists intend to do. Numerous studies have documented that in humans the coitus time since the moment the penis enters the vagina till ejaculation occurs, lasts on average some five minutes.

And here it's worth noting a very interesting and instructive fact: In man, the Baculum or penis bone has disappeared; it's present though in some primates to which we're closely related, and in many other mammals; whose function is to maintain erection during penetration, and even to achieve penetration without an erection, in order to prolong sexual intercourse and increase the possibilities of conception, because, usually, these are animals that live dispersed and couples only have sporadic encounters. It's been speculated that, in man, owing to the development of a mating system based on more stable relationships with specific females, to ensure the paternity of the offspring, which allows more frequent copulations, but of shorter duration, the existence of this bone became obsolete. And precisely this new sexual bonding scheme gave rise to the notion of female virginity to guarantee the origin of the children. The woman became the fundamental bulwark to ensure that only the best elements of the group had offspring. For millennia the system worked to achieve evolutionary advancement. Nowadays, in an egalitarian and mediocre society, such values are subject to scorn.

Once the reproductive age has passed, the sexual drive gradually diminishes given that it has already accomplished its assigned natural function. This is the reality, even though the braggarts who pretend to be very lascivious rear up. The problem is that there is a gigantic market to exploit one of the most difficult instincts to control, since man is one of the few animals that practices sex for pleasure, as a natural mechanism to keep the couple together until ensuring the self-sufficiency of the helpless offspring; nevertheless, it has been the perfect pretext to run wild. Sex Trade has become a lucrative business that generates unquantifiable profits. A whole paraphernalia has been created around sexual function; from sex toys and substances to improve performance, to the delirium of inventing creams to lighten the pussy, so that it doesn't look that dark! It's all about money. From there is born, exclusively, the perverse pretension to give this instinct the high rank that it does not naturally have. And if you don't believe it, ask the condom or aphrodisiac companies how high their revenue is. And if you are still not convinced, ask the poor rhinoceroses, turtles, whales, or gorillas, driven to the brink of extinction by the nonsense of a bunch of morons who seek a distorted pleasure beyond the natural, and the ambition of a herd of pigs who prey on them. Logically, to criticize it is vulgar, moralistic, prudish and whatever else comes to your mind. But wanting to approach everything from a sexual, corporeal perspective forgetting about the spiritual, is a sign of our bestial decadence; as in many ancient civilizations; dead today.

However, it's been taken as a symbol of "freedom", almost a distinctive characteristic of the "advanced" countries, even though it's nothing more than the reflection of a sick mind that seeks, at any cost, immediate physical pleasure, no matter how trivial it may be, to fill the existential vacuum of a meaningless life. The consequences of a dead soul.

But let's begin at the beginning. What is the function of sex? The answer is categorical: The reproduction of individuals to preserve the species. But Nature imposes one condition: Only the best members must reproduce in order to improve the genetic legacy. This is the basis of everything. From there we go to the level of sophistication of the species. Each one has developed the most favorable reproduction mechanisms for the circumstances and environment in which it thrives. The simplest ones use asexual procedures to multiply, such as a mere division of its own body. Just as functional complexity increases, other reproductive methods appear such as in beings that have in themselves both sexual components that are combined as part of their physiology. There are cases in which species of different levels harmonize to collaborate in the reproduction mechanisms, such as female fleas which, on lacking an endocrine system of their own, to activate their reproductive apparatus necessarily need to take advantage of the hormones in the blood of a host that is female and pregnant. And lastly, we come to mammals, the class to which we belong, where reproduction requires the intervention of two individuals of opposite sex. These are absolute facts perfectly established by Nature, and they do not admit the slightest discussion. Therefore, it's a stubbornness to pretend that the sexuality of different species can be compared or, worse, to fantasize that they can be interchangeable, just because we've come to conceive ourselves with the ability to play gods.

And already put on track, let's proceed to a still trickier topic; we'll surely see sparks. For the time being it is repeated ad nauseam as a dogma that men and women are equal, and that they have the same rights. The height of absurdity! Reality is overwhelming and irrefutable: From the genetic level, through the physical, physiological, psychological, emotional, social and even pathological, the differences between men and women are abyssal, and they determine the complementary function that belongs to each one to fulfill, to, together, enable the survival of the species. A revealing study published in a prestigious scientific journal established that the genetic difference between the chimpanzee and the man was of one per cent! And, even more shocking, that the genetic difference between man and woman, and between male and female chimpanzee was of two per cent! That is, the genetic difference was greater between genders than between species! Even so, in these pompous times of "Equality", to think the opposite is a true sacrilege.

Let's do a bit of history. One of the best kept secrets of the alleged movements for the emancipation of women is that feminism was initiated by men: The great entrepreneurs of the beginning of the Industrial Revolution. When production gained momentum and workforce became scarce and got expensive, they started a propaganda campaign for *"the liberation of women"*, which had the sole purpose of getting her out of the home, where she was *"the Lady of the house"*, to get more slaves for the factories, and thus cut the price of salaried work, and thereby lower their costs, and increase their proceeds. And women believed it. Today we have a world full of *"liberated"* female laborers, who work enslaving working days for ridiculous wages, whose homes are a disaster, and who even have to ask permission to go to the restroom. But it doesn't matter, despite the fact that the only thing they have failed to accomplish is to meet their most natural expectations, industrial progress keeps on flourishing, and the trap of feminism works wonders. The harsh reality is that, given the artificial role she is playing, today's woman is replaceable, disposable; even a man or a robot can do what she does! The times when she performed a crucial and irreplaceable function for the development of society are getting farther and farther away. Fecund, useful and committed to giving and protecting life, she was, furthermore, even without conducting a maternal role, creative and fruitful; and no matter how much they want to deny and discredit it, she was the nucleus, the solid pillar on which the social structure was sustained. When we take a look at ancient indigenous cultures, it's highly significant that their women regard the idea of gender equality not only as aberrant, but as an insult. And you have to see what an important role they play in their society. Within the current distorted perception of the meaning of progress and liberty, the great feminine aspirations are limited to being part of modernity, of the "great advance"; achieving, for instance, the fabulous dream of being a top executive, or better yet, the owner of a big company, it matters little that it's dedicated to filling the world with shit. This is what her ideals have been degraded to. To join the select group of "prominent entrepreneurs" whose sick ambition is insatiable; or of alleged artists who call grotesque things, innovation; of pseudo scientists who far from fostering knowledge, intellectual liberation, only serve as a foundation for consumerism, manipulation and enslavement of the individual, putting themselves at the service of whoever has the money to buy them; and of corrupt and arrogant politicians, full of hubris and greed for power. A whole fine collection of banal and sterile people; nefarious, noxious, useless beings…

At present, the manipulation of women has reached an obscene degree. They are compelled to be fashionable, to plaster makeup on, to lose their lives in a series of extravagant beauty rituals; the exploitation of femininity is quite a sweet deal. Worse still, the sophistication of advertising techniques has become so subtle, so sharp, that by using warped arguments that appear to be valid and reasonable, they have been convinced that it's their own decision, that, being so modern and progressive, the brilliant idea was born from them, even when it's just a vulgar domestication. It's not for nothing that companies' advertising expenses amount to exorbitant figures, with a disturbing percentage of commercials aimed at plunging them into the consumption of trinkets and trifles. The range of emotions permitted to people is increasingly getting narrower. It's revealing how the feminist groups, which do not hesitate to vociferate demanding all sorts of fictitious rights and liberties, faced with this shameful attack against the true freedom of women, keep a suspicious complicit silence. An all too ridiculous paradox is the criticism being made of women from other countries who refuse to accept the ostentatious modern ideology and prefer to preserve the ancient values of their cultures. For instance, the use of the burqa in the Muslim countries. As a reflection of their frustration and incapability to understand the mentality of women who are more connected to the real world, they reprove their behavior to the point of exhaustion and brand them as submissive, anachronistic, close-minded. They even assault them for not wearing a bikini on the beach. The truth is that with depilation, endless layers of make-up, hair dyed to hide grey hairs, very long, but fake, eyelashes and many other hideous impositions of fashion, the liberated modern women end up so unrecognizable, so covered as with the burqa, aggravated by the hypocritical boasting of pretending to be very free. Even when they are just as much as, or more manipulated than the women they criticize so much, they fiercely defend themselves with arguments that seem to be taken from a cosmetic commercial, you already know: "Because they're worth it".

And precisely, this frivolous and perverse subculture of veneration of physical beauty, regardless of it being artificial! has caused disastrous consequences. The cult of the body has become something obsessive, an addiction, even at the expense of health. The most deplorable thing is that the occasions in which physical beauty reflects the spiritual beauty of the individual are very rare. Regularly, people who let themselves be carried away by this fantasy are vain, hollow, haughty. Despite the fact that their sole attribute is a fortuitous circumstance of destiny that didn't cost them any effort to obtain, in their delusion they pretend that this converts them into special people, superior to the rest of mortals, therefore they deserve all the honors here, there and everywhere. The climax of such stupidity is the beauty pageants and the models, which denigrate the woman by turning her into an object, and they only serve to provide prostitutes for the moneyed; pricey and refined if you like, but, in the end, whores. It's no secret that many of them don't dislike, in the least, selling themselves to the highest bidder. The most tragic thing is that eventually reality prevails and unmasks all makeup, all falsehood. Our senseless quest for a beautiful ideal companion, even if she's bought, holds a great disappointment for us. As the grandparents warned: "Beauty wears off after a while; stupidity, they will take it to the grave".

Thus, we come to the relationship of the couple. Here it's indispensable to begin by defining several fundamental concepts to avoid misleading interpretations. Unlike what filmmakers and other show businessmen maintain, who only try to exploit the sentimentality of dupes to enrich themselves, love and infatuation are not the same thing. Even when they've wanted to trivialize love, there is an abyss between both of them; indeed, they are so utterly alien to each other that there is not the slightest difficulty in differentiating them:

Love means the renunciation of oneself, the total and unconditional surrender to an ideal, without asking or expecting anything in return, PERIOD! Very few people manage to reach this grace; especially in our civilization, increasingly egocentric and materialistic. It's characterized by the following:

1- It is a sublime feeling that is born from the soul, one of the pillars that support our human identity.

2- It gives us a sensation of imperturbable inner peace, even in the face of the most extreme situations, which allows the individual to liberate himself and achieve a great intellectual and spiritual harmony; to clarify his mind to focus his energy on being creative, on conducting some project.

3- It makes us understand that the most important thing is to give oneself and care for others, even before oneself. This, in addition to providing us with a beneficial well-being, spills out into our surroundings causing us enormous feelings of satisfaction and achievement for the work accomplished, which leads us to reach happiness, that serene emotion that, just like love, emerges from the depths of the soul, and with it, find a meaning in life.

4- From the above arises a commitment full of dedication, discipline and tenacity, which not only lasts a lifetime, but for which it's worth giving one's life.

5- LOVE IS NOT RECEIVED; LOVE CAN SOLELY BE GIVEN. There is nothing more incoherent and absurd than asking "to be loved".

Infatuation, quite on the contrary:

A- It's born from instinct, and has implicit a very strong sexual component, since it's bound to the most elemental needs, and it doesn't differ much from the seasonal rut of "irrational" animals, from which we boast to be very distant. Its PRIMORDIAL purpose is procreation, to ensure the survival of the species. PERIOD!

B- It obfuscates the mind, annulling reasoning, and it makes it impossible to look at the horizon. It prevents us from concentrating to develop our skills.

C- Originated in the reflex zones of the brain, it physiologically disturbs the body, causing anxiety, palpitations, sweating, and even the runs!

D- In serious, sickly cases, it imprisons the individual plunging him into passion, no escape possible, resulting in devastating consequences. Have you heard of murders of passion?

E- It makes the person egotistical, putting his welfare before everything else. Spiritually, it doesn't go beyond offering us fleeting and superficial emotions such as joy or its younger brother, contentment.

But let's elaborate a bit on the subject as it's key to make it quite clear that, despite the fact that we boast about calling "love" what we feel for our partner, and therefore we claim to be very romantic, sensitive and "loving", the infatuation that carries us away is a simple passion stemmed from sexual instinct and has ABSOLUTELY NOTHING to do with love. Its main foundation is the physical attraction for a person, to whom the glue of sexual pleasure holds us together. Nature itself has assigned it a duration of some three to four years, which suffices for the couple to reproduce, and the children they beget can grow up to fend for themselves, as it turns out that man, in a notable difference with all other members of the animal kingdom, is perhaps the most helpless and immature being at birth. Love and the relationship of the couple are INCOMPATIBLE because this one has as a foundation a diametrically opposite feeling. If they manage to weather the storm, survive the infatuation stage, they will be able to aspire to take refuge in affection, that placid sensation of feeling comfortable with each other. This is how simple the entire arcane and indecipherable mystery about the couple's relationship is synthetized; which has caused the ruthless deforestation and pollution of the earth, to produce books, movies and, even worse, songs and more songs where "Love" is venerated, with which merchants exploit the trivial sappiness of so many morons who, in this costume of romantics and moved to tears, feel hyper humans. But despite poets, philosophers and Quixotes, reality becomes patent in all of its harshness. It's very significant that in "ancient and obsolete" times they had the clear conviction that, with the passage of the years, engrossed in routine and the relentless monotony of everyday life, it ended up not existing a substantial difference between the quality of the relationship and cohabitation of a marriage "for love" and one between "not so in love" ones, and even one forced by agreements or out of convenience. And they considered it ridiculous to want to claim that the former were happier or more prosperous. In the end, the couple's relationship ends up being worn out by the same factors, and biochemical ones are, inevitably, an essential part of it. The hormones of "passion" are also depleted. That's why, appealing to centenarian wisdom, marriages were arranged by parents, who had a clearer view to provide their children with a more promising future.

Here we're faced with a crucial juncture of our time. Accustomed to demanding rights, we vociferate in indignation to defend the power we have to choose whatever we feel like. Nevertheless, we forget that to know how to choose we must first prepare and learn to discern. Having the possibility of choosing, without knowing how to choose, is a thousand times worse than not having the opportunity to do so! And in the vast majority of cases, it brings disastrous results. A very crude example to illustrate the question: If, from amongst the countless assortment of available photographic cameras we wanted to choose one, without knowing or understanding the features of each one, in order to know which one would be the most convenient for our needs, the probabilities that we select one that does NOT serve us are extremely high. The panorama changes drastically if we resort to a person who knows the subject for advice, expounding our needs to him. This applies to many fields of life such as setting personal goals, or the education of children.

These days, despite the ostentation we make of having an avant-garde ideology, free from all ties, and with full maturity to select our spouse, couples proliferate with increasing frequency who, with trumpets and drums, completely in love, marry the "Love of their Life", which they themselves chose, only to end up, after the brief period of infatuation, divorcing on very bad terms, and, on occasion, hating each other to death for "the rest of their lives". And it's just that, in our materialistic and superfluous society, our guide is not spiritual values but physical appearance and money. Thus, we "fall madly in love" with a physically beautiful person, in spite of the fact that, spiritually, she is someone banal, devoid of ideals and incapable of committing herself. Logically, the results are more than predictable.

We also come across the classic couple of oldies who boast of having loved each other their whole lives, and who consider themselves an example of the idyllic "Eternal Love". In reality, they only managed to go from infatuation to placid habit, and from there to the primeval fear of the unknown, of change, of leaving their comfort zone; conveniently helped by the decrease in sexual appetite, once the reproductive phase is over. Now, without the sexual instinct prodding you, and with the emotional maturity and the intellectual capacity to weigh conveniences, it's far easier to maintain a long-term relationship based on gratitude, solidarity, and memories. All of that without mentioning the influence and commitment that children, if there were any, generate. Unfortunately for dreamers, nothing in Nature indicates that our fate is the fairytale fantasy of couples who live together forever, wrapped in the "Love of their Lives". This artificial and irrational conception was concocted as an instrument to control and take advantage of the masses. But don't tell the hopeless romantics, there is danger that they might even throw themselves off a bridge.

Such is the case when a toxic component is added to this "love" potion, that embroils things in an infernal way: Passion. This is nothing more than the unbridled infatuation of someone incapable of controlling himself, that is, a damn stupid guy. But it has been exacerbated by romantic novels and fairytales that have created fictitious and, frankly, idiotic stories, in which a passionate relationship is frozen in time, when one or both protagonists die, "Eternal Love" remaining idealized, and insinuating that a relationship of this kind is the only thing that is worth as a goal of life. With all malice they omit the reasoning that, simply, it was a relationship that didn't have the opportunity to mature, to have the natural evolution that, with time, routine, and on appeasing, or extinguishing, the fire of passion, it would be led, perhaps, to a heartbreak. Torrid romances filled with passion for eternity are mere malicious fabrications vilely invented by the entertainment industry. Sadly, the incapability to adapt to reality is what drives the unbridled lover to suicide. So it goes, one less dumbass.

And so, for centuries we have worn ourselves out emotionally, seeking tirelessly our chimeric "significant other", our "soulmate". But the true disaster came when this ardent desire joined forces with religion and it was established a whole series of norms and traditions of what behavior and life as a couple should be. Matrimony and monogamy were, then, born with the supposed purpose of providing protection to women and children, and at the same time to control our savage instincts and our most unhinged passions. Again, the problem was that Nature was not taken into account, and they wanted to dodge the important fact that the most natural and common practice of social behavior throughout all of human history was precisely polygamy, that is, the relationship of a man with several women, and it was the key factor that allowed the human species to survive and thrive on the face of the earth. Genetic tracking has demonstrated that, until a few millennia ago, all human progeny descended from a limited number of males. By artificially basing the social structure on the flimsy foundation of monogamy, due to irrational religious considerations or untenable moral rules, such as the alleged influence of malevolent demoniacal forces, numerous conflicts that are truly laughable have arisen. Perhaps one of the thorniest is that of infidelity. The usual so-called "experts" try to explain this conduct in men as a psychological mechanism to compensate for complexes and insecurities in their masculinity. Please, PLEASE!! We insist on molding reality to our prejudices. Man is by nature polygamous, PERIOD! Living in an aggressive and unforgiving environment, and provided with limited resources, the social structure of polygamy favored that small groups, composed of a man and several women as a single family, had more children, and more mothers in charge of their care, especially because not all of them procreated, increasing the possibilities that some of the kids managed to survive, in order to contribute to the progress of the collectivity. As chores were diluted, uneasiness and dread decreased, and the results were maximized. It's a real atrocity that, out of coarse ignorance and unwholesome opportunism, they want to ignore the primeval instinctive origin of this behavior which, despite the multitude of laws that have condemned it throughout the ages, stigmatizing it as sinful and immoral, almost inspired by Satan, it refuses to disappear, since it derives from the simple adaptation of the Human Being to the rules of Nature. It's even been disparaged by labeling it "machismo". Of course, this approach is anathema as it contradicts all the "great advances" we have achieved in matters of "gender equality", and its supporters deserve nothing less than the stake. In contrast, with an ideology manipulated to the point of incoherence, as a product of our reclusion in an increasingly sick and degraded synthetic world, in "advanced" countries female infidelity has increased; whose main causal arguments are the intolerable "lack of love" and attention of an egotistic, indolent or wicked man; or judging it as an act of vindication of the fictitious equality of rights that radical feminism has so much demanded and considered as a pending issue to be resolved, long overdue. In tune with the ideology of our times, there is a whole generation of egocentric people who think that the world is there to please them. Such reasonings, grounded on artificial premises without any biological foundation, have complicated the cohabitation of couples and are affecting the vital fabric of a society that, in addition, is in check as a consequence of its "laudable technological achievements" that have inflicted so much damage to the planet. Our estrangement from Nature is taking its toll on us.

And it's not about having submissive and enslaved women, whose only function be reproduction, but about having a society that is HEALTHY, judicious and useful for Nature. The ultimate goal involves the care and education of the progeny, and the creation of a milieu conducive to its development. It's worth noting a very evident circumstance: We all know the spinster aunt in charge of the grandparents, or the mistress of this or that one who never formed a family, or the uncle who never married, and lived for his job. In the same way as in other mammalian societies, where certain males, due to incompetence, do not get mates, or some females do not procreate offspring, in human society there are also many individuals who are born without the aptitudes to be parents, and we're not speaking of bodily factors; by nature, they are destined to perform secondary functions. When we want to forcibly integrate them into the social scheme conceived by our ridiculous pretension of creating an egalitarian society, making them feel compelled to form a family, without being fitted for it, severe disorders are caused to these people and, at the same time, to the entire community. We had not mentioned the advantages of polygamy, had we? It is here where the ostentatious and arbitrary projects of social progress have miserably failed. And all of this has nothing to do with moral, religious or rights issues. It's Nature in its purest expression. Unfortunately, even science, which today has even gotten into the bed, and of which we brag so much as bearer of truth, has done its bit to muddle the natural social order. Thus, we have renowned scholars who, despite the fact that they knew they were under the influence of psychotropic substances, they have dared to invent psychedelic theories about human behavior, which we must unarguably accept as veridical. No Mister Freud, you are totally wrong! Women do not wish to have a penis nor do they get a complex about not having one. In fact, women also have a penis, tiny, but in the end a penis, the clitoris, which essentially works under the same physiological mechanism as the masculine penis. For your information, sir, it also occurs the "uncanny coincidence" that women like the dick being inserted in them, that's what Nature programmed them for; and how they enjoy it! Anatomy books state it clearly and concisely: The vagina is the ideal receptacle to receive the penis. This anatomical compatibility facilitates fecundation, providing the perfect mechanism to achieve the reproduction of the species. And in passing it treats us with a good orgasm, if we stop believing myths and learn how they actually work. And speaking of the puerile and apocalyptic conflicts of the couple, there are few that cannot be solved with some good big licks on the clitoris. Life is ephemeral. Let's stop wasting it in bullshit!

Let's move on to a hotter topic. And to begin with, however senseless and incredible it may seem, it's necessary to clarify that, by irrefutable designs of Nature, only women can get pregnant! Solely women were granted the attribute of procreating children, an essential role for society. Even more absurd is the fact that many feminists regard this as a burden to which they were unjustly condemned, and it represents a shameful symbol of sexual discrimination. We've even made pregnancy a disease! The main point is that this, what formerly was considered a privilege, entails a huge responsibility which, today, has been taken lightly and even scorned, causing serious problems. One of the most far-fetched is intentional abortion as a solution to an "oversight". And here it makes no sense to exempt oneself by blaming man, woman is the one who gets pregnant; the privilege and the obligation fall to her. Moreover, given the vast availability and publicity that is being made today of contraceptive methods to prevent unwanted pregnancy, there shouldn't even be a need for it! The eventuality of getting pregnant for not having taken the necessary precautions reflects a supreme lack of commitment and a huge cowardice in the face of a transcendental duty. It's aberrant the defense that feminists make of an alleged right to treacherously kill a helpless, vulnerable being, in order to correct an irresponsible conduct, and to suppose that the rights of an indolent woman are more important than those of a being who didn't even ask to be conceived. In Nature, it's a failure as a woman. It's argued that she is the owner of her body and can do whatever she wants with it; true, as the greengrocers in the market say, "she can spread her legs all around town", but she cannot dispose of the life of another being. Endless excuses have been concocted: That, being an embryo, he has no consciousness; that his heart is not beating yet; whether he will be viable or not. They are mere fallacious and grotesque pretexts to justify negligence and even perversity. If you kill a caterpillar, you're killing a future butterfly, if you kill an embryo, you're killing a future person, it's that simple. This is not a legal, philosophical or political question, nor does it have to do with the idiotic concept of sin wielded by religion, nor with moral and puritanical censures, this is, simply, a biological cycle, a reality, PERIOD! If we interrupt this cycle at any of its stages, we're impeding the development of the being to which it will finally give rise. It's like arguing that we can kill a baby but not an adult because, given the extreme bodily differences, they are not the same kind of being. That is to say that embryo, child and elderly person are not stages of the same individual! If we're going to accept the abortion of a defenseless and innocent being as a right, agreed! But then let's call things by their real name and accept murder as something normal; and let's stop complaining about so much violence that our society suffers. Enough of playing the victims. Let's mature and cope with the consequences of our own actions.

And yes, in Nature, the ultimate goal of the couple relationship is the procreation of competent and healthy children to continue the everlasting cycle of life. Parenthood is the stage where our responsibilities reach their climax. Even though, in Nature, every parent prepares his offspring to face the real world; we, as a supposedly superior species, cannot limit ourselves to satisfy a basic animal need where only instinct and biology are involved, but aspire to have a more profound and transcendental existence, lived with the mind and the soul. To have a child not only to care for and train him, but to instruct, to guide him. Have you ever wondered why babies are so adorable? Yes, once again, survival. It's a simple natural mechanism to motivate parents to protect them, to love them. With their curiosity, their lack of prejudice, their good faith, their ability to enjoy simple things, they give us the opportunity to be enthralled by perceiving the fascination of the world through their eyes, to walk the path again, learn to live anew; and delight ourselves in the experience of seeing them grow and become Human Beings. The arrival of a child gives us the opportunity to intimately incorporate ourselves into Cosmos which, thereby, confers on us the honorable task of committing ourselves to a very minuscule part of it itself; a minute gear embedded in its grandiose and perennial machinery, to whom we must protect and educate to integrate him into the harmony of the Universe. It's not an object of our property intended to please our whims and complexes. Children do not belong to us!

However, in our deteriorated society, difficulties begin with irresponsible parents who do not motivate their children to be better, as it entails the obligation that they too must try to be better, and that's an effort they are not willing to make. On the other hand, there are the men who due to apathy, ineptitude or cowardice do not play the role that Nature has assigned them as guides and managers for the welfare of the family, leaving the development of children in charge of the woman, hiding behind a cynical mask of ridiculous liberalism. Do you remember how in polygamy people unfit to be parents conduct secondary functions? All of this has given rise to countless conflictive situations such as that of single mothers, quite a current trend, who, on having children without a father, seriously affect the prosperity of the children; and I am not referring to economic matters. There is no way of excluding the fundamental role played by the presence of a father as a helmsman within the family. But it has almost become customary to have children as if they were toys; without weighing whether one has the resources to provide them with what is necessary for their physical welfare, and to give them the opportunity to have a full intellectual and spiritual development. And so, we see thousands of refugees who, deceitfully invoking human rights, flee carrying in tow a bunch of kids brought into the world without the slightest consideration or compassion, knowing full well that they are destined for misery and exploitation. Procreating children irrationally, worse than animals, without having the least economic, family or patrimonial stability, and a minimum of security, constitutes a serious crime against humanity, and must be punished as such!

In the ostentatious gallery of the magnificent advances achieved to foster the respect for gender equality is the obligation to constantly specify the gender of the subjects, under penalty of offending the great libertarian values of our avant-garde modern civilization, and being immediately stigmatized as discriminator, misogynist and regressive person. But it's an aberration to a superlative degree that, in order to conform to the new norms of manipulated comportment, the effectiveness of an essay be taken off, and even literary composition be disrupted; in addition to deforming grammar, to enshroud a terrifying ignorance. Soon we'll be talking about the dentist and the dentistress, or the youngster and the youngstress, and there won't be lacking he who have the great creativity to use them in poetry! This tendency to abuse language as a tool to evade ourselves from our complexes and prejudices is also observed in the trend of using terms of "tremendousness" to rate any trifle. Like this, the performance of a pseudo artist can be grandiose, or a wedding dress, marvelous, and even a building can be magnificent. And we ran out of words, with what adjectives are we going to describe an eclipse, an aurora borealis or the sight of a galaxy. So much stupidity borders on the nauseating. But it's a mortal sin to hurt the susceptibility of the "intrepid" reformers and innovators. To me… I don't give it a shit!

And already pissed off, let's meddle into another subversive controversy. What a damned habit! Let's reflect a little on homosexuality. The first thing that becomes evident is the overwhelming publicity campaigns to persuade, and induce tolerance for this behavior with the pretension that it be considered something normal and worthy of acquiescence. The unusual squandering of resources, the vast dissemination, ostensible or surreptitious, and the pertinacious proposal that its rejection is a prejudiced affront, imply an obscure sponsorship that seems to respond to warped interests, with the intention of undermining the foundations of human society. It's not something natural or spontaneous. Evil tongues speculate that it's a Machiavellian plan to reduce world population, on the logic that dick against dick or pussy against pussy, it won't go beyond a good rubbing, without procreating anything. In the faculty of medicine, we studied it objectively as one of the deviations of sexual behavior. Nevertheless, what was then something perfectly established, has become a real mess by pretending that all these behaviors are expressions of freedom, and must be considered as "natural sexual preferences". To back it up, they argue that no brain defect or genetic damage has been found. But neither does the gene for homosexuality exist, to have a real foundation. As an illuminating comparison, let's consider the case of patients with epilepsy. According to statistics, in ninety eight percent of cases it's diagnosed as idiopathic, what in plain language means that its causes are unknown. In other words, despite all the studies conducted on these patients, neither a triggering factor nor any trace of damage or defects in their brains is located; and yet, even when the patient should be classified as healthy, we cannot suspend the treatment, because he would HAVE A SEIZURE AGAIN! And seizures cannot be considered as something normal! He needs medication for life to control the crisis or he's going to progressively deteriorate with each one of them, until becoming mentally retarded or, in severe cases, dying. Even though his brain appears to be completely healthy, the person is ill! It's exactly the same case of a homosexual; even if shoddy politicians and super liberals kick up a fuss.

What is important is that the behavioral disorder of homosexuality is not limited to a disturbed preference for individuals of the same sex. Throughout history it has been characterized by a volatile temperament where sex has a preponderant role. He also suffers from an extreme emotional lability, being susceptible to excesses such as drug dependency. He is, besides, distinguished by depraved conducts such as transvestism, which reaches grotesque degrees, a sordid life, sometimes full of vices, and a lack of control that leads to violence and pathological passion. Crimes of passion between homosexuals are counted amongst the most sanguinary. But homosexuality is not the only case of perversion of sexual behavior, there are sexually sick people who prefer to have sex with animals, with cadavers, and voyeurs who even look for lovers to their partners, to spy on them when they have sexual intercourse with someone else, because only in this way they manage to experience sexual pleasure. And there are also pedophiles, most of whom, no matter how much we insist on denying or ignoring it, are first of all homosexuals, but whose preference is for minors, coming, in truly aberrant cases, as far as wanting to have sex with babies. Although, in our supposed avant-garde liberalism, we want to pretend that all these sickly attitudes are expressions of natural sexuality and must be respected, reality is that they are people who were born with mental disorders that lead them to unacceptable pathological behaviors. Their brain was born with a functional disturbance, it's sick! These ailments are comparable to those of people who were born with a cleft lip, or without an arm or an ear, or even with Down syndrome. It all due to congenital abnormalities, even though contemporary science doesn't allow us yet to precisely establish the cause and the location of said alteration. If these patients have any right, like any other patient, it's to have access to an adequate treatment, and even if it's not possible to cure them, at least try to palliate their innate problem insomuch as possible, to help them cope with it; much like providing a prosthesis to an amputee. But it's absurd to demand that, for instance, patients suffering syphilis, tuberculosis or AIDS have the freedom to spread their disease and harm society under the pretext that they too are within their right. An ancient proverb says quite to the purpose: "The sole dictatorship that peoples accept is sanitary dictatorship". It's, absolutely, the same situation of mental disorders that affect behavior, like schizophrenia or homosexuality. No matter how much we want to refute it, they are congenital pathological conditions that alter the affective abilities and must be considered for what they are: A true tragedy; since they're going to prevent the individual from enjoying a full life, and they'll affect his expectations of being happy. They are not special attributes, much less is it a condition for which an apology must be made, and be awarded with exclusive rights, or even more, consider it as a new gender! How far has gone the twisted mentality of a sick and decadent society that is incapable of facing reality. Under the most elementary logic, why are we going to consider some disorders of sexual behavior as "sexual preferences", and we're going to demonize and punish others as criminal and depraved? If, in their deranged mind, for a homosexual pedophile, sex with children, or for a rapist, sex with violence, are their "correct" conception of what having sexual relations is; don't do they also have the right to have their "preferences" respected, and that we consider them as a separate "category"? How we like to play the dumbass!

The natural repudiation of societies towards these individuals has nothing to do with prejudices or demoniacal influences, as the tiresome propaganda tries to make us believe. Let's situate ourselves again in reality. If we saw a deformed, enormous or strange being coming towards us, say a huge hairy beast or a mythical Cyclops, that damned giant with a single eye on the forehead, before we could even think about it, our instincts would immediately arouse an IRREPRESSIBLE response of defense, of rejection, to flee or fight to confront a potential danger. This uncontrollable reflex is one of the basic resources with which Nature provided us to protect ourselves from the unknown and to be able to survive. An irrefutable testimony? Restrain the reflex of closing your eyes and protecting yourself with the hands when an object is thrown at your face. The aversion to behaviors that are judged as depraved is not a question of intolerance or morality, it's just an expression of the most fundamental self-preservation instinct with which communities protect themselves from conducts perceived as pernicious, since homosexual unions would be infertile and they would finish off the species. As simple as that. It's a natural law of survival. Homosexuality is just a disease, the product of a congenital functional defect and its consequent physiological disorders. The popular wisdom of the people of remote villages where they still enjoy of a keen common sense, expresses it in a very plain and categorical way, tinged with compassion: "That poor man was born with the wires crossed". As a devastating blow to our pretentious hubris, this indisputable example attests to the fragility of the super powerful human mind, which we almost consider divine. It's revealing and shocking the fact that a simple change in the biochemistry of the brain can cause it catastrophic disturbances; the mere lack of an insignificant substance can turn the King of Creation into an imbecile. Throughout history, very few patients with mental disorders have managed to stand out, and their life has been a tragic unabated struggle against their adverse health conditions, of which they became aware and exerted themselves to overcome them, they didn't consider them a virtue to be boasted. It's not about tolerance, it's about having the guts to confront reality.

Hypocritically we like to brag about being a super tolerant and compassionate civilization. However, the dire consequences of our contrived and opportunistic magnanimity are perfectly illustrated by the disastrous case of the diabetic clubs. Founded to motivate solidarity and emotional support among these patients, to cope with their illness, they promoted sharing time together, what fostered the formation of couples with the same genetic defect, substantially increasing the possibility that the children of these marriages developed diabetes. As a result of a hasty and negligent intervention, succeeding generations were condemned to suffer from the disease. Even more grotesque is the reckless bet of opening up the possibility for homosexuals to be able to adopt children to satisfy their emotional needs, as if they were marionettes on sale. Invoking fraudulent privileges instituted by our pathetic hyper humanism, they intend to grant them a right for which Nature has already determined their incompetence. Here it's key to make it clear that the homosexual is born, not made; it's an innate disorder. The problem is that, due to massive manipulation, homosexuality has become a fad that must be joined regardless of the consequences. The avant-garde novelty is that, today, at any age, "queerness" can take hold of anyone, and there are already hordes of them. Pseudo homosexuality has nothing to do with a congenital alteration but with a disorder of the soul, the product of an unhinged life in the "Artifiture", as my father called it; the dazzling world of cement, plastic and pollutants, where the deranged anonymous crowds get rotten, which has profoundly disrupted our Being. This morbid indoctrination is, no more, no less, the same thing that leads them to get tattooed, to shave their heads bald or to dye their mop of hair in colors; to become goth, zombie or vampire, etcetera, etcetera, etcetera. And that without having yet talked about the LGBTIQ, let alone the WXYZ. The table is set for the taming of the imbeciles. In the old days, grandparents used to say that each head was a world; those were, then, the times when the world had a head. Today they all dress alike, behave alike and degrade themselves alike. If a fool dyes his hair green, there will always be a bunch of idiots who follows him to, in this way, feel free. To emancipate themselves from social bonds! Such overwhelming coincidences are just the sad reflection of a frightful and grotesque taming. And for those braggarts who swank about being very tolerant and liberal, a reflection: If we so much support "natural demonstrations", why not simply let Nature act, and allow the Ebola virus to survive, for example, or the plague that in a single month killed thirty million bastards, helping to control population and giving the poor planet a healthy respite. Or tolerate cannibalism, which is another natural mechanism of population control that diminishes the human pressure on environmental resources. Of all those liberals who are champions of tolerance, how many of you sign up to make a law, the natural laws?

The much-vaunted thesis that sex is the force that drives the world is a big lie. Suffice it to review history a little bit to realize that, for instance, Pasteur, Beethoven, Einstein and so many others personalities who made the great contributions that have transformed humankind, in that creative moment the sole thing they were not thinking about was sex. So, the next time a moron comes at you with that silly tale, don't take him so seriously; you can be certain he only wants to sucker you into selling you something. In conclusion: What is different is not equal, and being different is not being inferior! How irrational that there be a need to define and elucidate such a forceful reality; it's spine-chilling the degree to which we've lost the most basic common sense. It's essential to say things the way they are, without taking into account political considerations and idiotic social trends; men and women are not equal, much less do they have the same rights. Nature has already established, indubitably, the differences and the complementary role that each one performs in society. This is not an ideological matter, it's a real fact. The mere pretension of wanting to rebut it, is already a stubbornness. Using the most primordial reasoning, we have to question ourselves: If both sexes must be equal and have the same functions, what, then, do two sexes exist for!?

That sexuality is everything in life; that there must be "gender equality"; that homosexuality is a "sexual preference"; yeah, I bet so! And your Popsicle… What flavor?

CHAPTER V

JUMP MONKEY, JUMP, OR THEY GET YOU CAGED!

The Winding Road of the Baby Beast

Eat, Shit and Sleep; he only dedicated himself to that. He spent most of the day sleeping, resting, saving energy to be able to make his quotidian nighttime fuss. Already in the blackness, deranged by his ceaseless heartrending screams, we were on the verge of becoming zombies. But when all seemed lost, things unexpectedly changed. Little by little he was entering reality, sleep took its rhythm and hunger its place; he even started pooping when he should. There is strong scientific evidence that, during the first three months of life, the baby thinks that he's still inside his mother's womb. And it's precisely from this discordance with reality that so many "survivalistic" problems arise; already since then the mess begins. Now he's grown a little, he learns by playing, he amuses himself throwing big punches against whatever gets in his way; he begins to run, to poke around. Nevertheless, it's useless to try to make him to see reason or understand a refusal, he's more stubborn than a mule; he wants to do whatever he likes. It would certainly be futile to try to converse with him about philosophy, science, art. It's going to pass a very long time before I can even try it. In the early stages of existence, the priority is to learn to survive. He's already spent the first phase of his life as any animal cub. He is currently in the stage of the Eating, Shitting and Playing, which is going to increase his physical capacities, for the struggle for subsistence. At his age of five, the first sketches of an intellectual takeoff begin to appear, he's training his wings to fly. He still has to go through the Dine, Crap and Screw; the life of the DCS (*decease*), which revolves around the reproduction instinct. The last animal stage of our development, which the vast majority will never surpass. But let's trust that, finally, he manages to reach the human level of the Exploring, Feeling and Thinking. We must be patient. The time will come when he becomes aware of the Universe, that his spirit matures, awakes; perhaps when adolescence ends; with any luck, on turning ten; I hope to be alive then; and I'm going to talk to him about the mind and the soul, about Nature and the meaning of life, of death. For now, I just have to love him…

We're not born human! What a forceful and irrefutable truth. It suffices to devote a little of time studying the behavior of our children, of kids, to comprehend it. At birth we're nothing more than animals, like any other of those who inhabit the globe. Our behavior betrays us outright. But we're getting ahead of ourselves. Just as the idea of god had to be clarified, it's indispensable to define precisely: What is a Human Being, or what is it that makes us human? What is man like in his natural state before he's manipulated, or domesticated? We have millennia cowardly postponing this paramount obligation so as not to confront our preconceptions, our traumas, our mediocrity. To avoid committing ourselves, we make, without any foundation, the idiotic assumption that we are all born Human Beings. But reality unequivocally contradicts our optimistic conclusions; even worse, it demonstrates that our intellectual development has stagnated. But in order to solve a problem, it's indispensable, first of all, to recognize that the problem exists.

And we start again. On what can we base our judgement to establish the defining parameters? On religion? With the ravages it has caused, and the futility that it has shown throughout the centuries; always changing and malleable according to the times and likings. And in the last case, which of them, that is not corrupted to favor the twisted desires of its leaders? On philosophy? With the complexes and prejudices that overwhelm man; with the fears, vanities and ineptitudes that obfuscate our understanding? The narrow reaches of so many cheap digressions have already done too much damage as to believe that they are going to light the way. On science? Focused on the domestication of man and to ensure the economic benefit of the highest bidder. Even drug traffickers have scientists at their service to create new drugs, more potent and addictive. And not to mention the "eminent scientists" working for the arms manufacturers. The only real possibility that remains is to return to our roots, to Nature; tangible, authentic, constant, whose validity is perennial and universal; and it's not conditional to the discretion of rotten politicians, imbecilic fashions or stupid redeemers. To define ourselves and find a solution to our existential conflicts, we must read the book of Nature, and put aside the one of man.

Thus, the key question is: In Nature, what does differentiate the Human Being from the other beings that form the animal kingdom? The answer is categorical and quite simple, two "very tiny" attributes: The mind and the soul. Nothing more! They're the sole things that separate us from the beasts; and they enable us to define with absolute and irrefutable precision what a Human Being is: Someone with the imperative need of using his intellect and sensibility as much as breathing and more than eating. To calm his disquiet and his urge to find a meaning to his existence, reflection, understanding and knowledge are essential to him; but equally emotions, desires, ideals and, above all, freedom and the communion with Nature, as beginning and end. Here, more than ever, it gains importance the millenary and transcendental phrase: *Consciousness determines being.* The human condition is achieved, solely, by taking cognizance of oneself and of our relationship with the Universe. The key point is that, at birth, these qualities are latent, immature, unfinished, and in many cases, unfortunately, absent; initially they're not functional, unlike the heart or the lungs. We have the innate potential but it's not going to develop by itself, it's indispensable to cultivate it, something like learning to walk. As our intellectual and spiritual faculties are perfected, we ascend the scale of consciousness until reaching the human category. The ability for discernment, properly human, only develops in the last stage of the evolution of the intellect. And this must be our purpose in life, to seek spiritual and mental development over the physical, in order to make the most of the distinctive aptitudes with which Nature endowed us. If we don't use them, we are condemning ourselves to an animal existence. Our obsession with progress and scientific advancement has led us to believe that we can afford the luxury of losing our natural qualities, and replace them with technology, but that has only distanced ourselves from our human condition. The Homo Faber who, trapped in an artificial world, ends up turning into an artificial being, not human.

From the above it derives that we have the possibility of living in three ways:

1- Corporeally: By satisfying only physical needs; the life of the DECEASE: Dine, Crap and Screw. That is, just like a pig does.

2- Mentally: By considering the situations coldly and mechanically, as if we were robots.

3- Spiritually: By increasing our sensations and emotions. Expanding the soul.

If we manage to reconcile these last two, our horizon broadens out in a formidable way. It's fundamental to specify that intelligence alone is not enough!; for the simple logic of the essential factors that constitute the human being; it's also indispensable a good dose of common sense, of reasonableness, but above all a great emotional maturity is required, what today is ostentatiously called "emotional intelligence", which determines the self-sufficiency to control our conduct, plan our actions, solve difficulties and relate to our environment. Hence, the pretentious tests to evaluate the "intelligence quotient" prove to be stupid, because rather than providing a true assessment of a person's performance, they have only served as a pretext for a bunch of imbeciles to feel superior.

One can be the most intelligent of them all, but if he doesn't learn to adequately use such aptitude, he won't go beyond being a mediocre or, if worst comes to worst, a criminal who only uses his abilities to harm the others. Thus, we have a group of morbidly obese men who consider themselves geniuses because they have a high IQ and excel at playing chess, but they aren't good at anything else, not even at taking care of their own body; or a person capable of doing amazing calculations using only his mind, but with a serious emotional disorder that renders him incapable to have a satisfactory social relationship. It's important to point out that common sense is simply the use of the most primary reasoning to discern and evaluate the circumstances in which we develop; and it's very remarkable that the reactions of various individuals, even living in isolated places or in different eras, are very similar if not identical; this is because they originate in the intrinsic instinctual regions of the Being, in the vital zones of the human brain where the most primeval reflexes are stored, which are common to all, that is precisely why it's called common sense! It's therefore a fundamental defense weapon to be able to survive. It's neither subject to philosophical dissertations nor to the free will of each one. It doesn't stem from customs or stereotyped social guidelines, as they have perversely wanted to discredit it. Quite the contrary, those are precisely which have caused its deterioration. As societies have become "civilized", artificial behaviors have been implanted to "favor social coexistence", which on getting us away from our natural origin have annulled our most elementary instincts. The mediocre man needs laws that show him the way and forge a destiny for him because he doesn't have the capability to be free and to invent one of his own. With the manipulation of the individual reaching abominable extremes, without opposing the slightest resistance to decerebration, a distorted perception of duty has been conditioned, which obligates the individual to obey stupid laws, nullifying the most basic sound judgment and dignity. For the time being, it's the least common of senses; and its near death is frightfully patent. Two clear examples: Have you seen the hordes of people huddling together like cattle at the crossings of the street corners because the pedestrian traffic light signals them STOP? And even if no vehicle comes through the streets, not even in the distance, no one dares to disobey it! Still more aberrant, the soldier who is capable of committing atrocities only because he was ordered to do so. Someone who let himself be bossed around in such a grotesque way, does not reach the category of Human Being.

It's indispensable to understand that the brain is the infrastructure on which the two essential pillars whose functions determine human identity rest: The mind, where intellectual activity takes place, and the soul or spirit, where emotional processes are carried out. What fosters intellectual development? One of the most crucial elements has been language, which, absolutely, didn't appear out of nowhere nor is it made randomly and senselessly. Just like science, it was born from a logical interpretation of reality, due to the need to express and transmit accurate ideas; it was not just about saying words like an idiot, as we do today. It was essentially a communication tool to enable survival. Just in case we have forgotten, for the primitive man, staying alive was his primordial concern. However, over time, it had a far more momentous function: On making possible the generation and coordination of ideas, it gave rise to the evolution of the brain. When thinking is activated, mechanisms that create new neuronal connections are triggered, which enable it to develop ever more complex concepts. As language became broader and more sophisticated to describe an increasingly vast world, mental capacity increased, creating more intricate notions and the consequent need to express them, in a virtuous circle that further fueled intellectual growth; until reaching abstract thinking, which is the highest function that human reasoning performs. One of the great challenges that particularly favors this advance is the learning of another language, which not only increases his provision of new words, but on having access to the mentality of other societies, the individual is confronted with another conception of the world, another perspective from which to interpret it, with another way of expressing ideas, making his own universe expand. That's why the aim of many countries to establish a single official language is a serious attack against the intellect of their own citizens. The most calamitous consequence of not promoting language proficiency is that people fail to develop the capability to define their own ideas, or to express their thoughts, let alone their feelings. The most scatterbrained try to impress using stilted phrases without articulating concrete ideas. A limited vocabulary produces limited minds. Hence also the concern about current technology, which, for the sake of a distorted efficiency and an irrational struggle against time, tries to "simplify" language more and more, to better communicate! Scientific studies show that nowadays young people use just forty words, most of them distorted, to communicate with each other. Added to this is the usage of arbitrary abbreviations and omissions in text messages. Have you seen, by pure chance, the funny little faces of the stupefying e-mojis? Language being one of the main mechanisms for the intellectual progress of the individual, with our negligence in the face of its degradation, we're building a generation of morons. In fact, we already have the pompous generation I, because they were born with the internet, as if this were a very commendable attribute; in reality we should call them I for imbeciles. They're convinced that technology is the maximum; the universal panacea that will make us evolve. And very much in spite of the opinion of certain Nobel Prize winners in literature and renowned poets who, in a presumptuous attitude of boastful ultraliberalism, pretend to discard even the most minimal trace of grammar and orthography to, supposedly, "liberate the expression of the human soul". A rich and well-structured language serves to clarify ideas, to deepen reasoning, and thus improve reflection and comprehension. Periods, commas, adjectives, adverbs, were creations of great talents. Similarly, today they brag that the computer is essential to improve education and increase intelligence. We want to forget that the genius is not he who learns to use a computer, but he who created it. Its use has been simplified so much that it's within the reach of any fool. But it's promoted as the great advance of modernity trying to deny its negative effects, some of them truly alarming, such as exposing us to a proven carcinogenic electromagnetic field, mainly with the state-of-the-art wireless accessories, or permanently affecting visual acuity, and, worse still, causing serious damage to the development of hand-eye coordination; one of the great determinants of intellectual evolution, which gave rise to what is, perhaps, the most preeminent and genuine demonstration of the human soul: Art.

To accurately assess esthetic manifestations, it's imperative to place ourselves in the era in which they were created. It all began with the fascinating attempts at cave paintings as primeval artistic expression of cavemen who, despite being engaged in an arduous struggle for survival that is unimaginable these days, they took the time to capture ideas and feelings that unsettled their spirit, seeking to expand the boundaries of human sensibility. Apogee was then reached with the unbelievable perfection of realism, followed by ethereal romanticism and the masterful impressionist attempt to capture movement, fleeting time, till reaching the enigmas of surrealism that transported us into the realm of dreams. Today modern art has fallen into grotesqueness and banality to satisfy commercial interests, fashion is: "Let the spectator imagine whatever he wants, while I play the asshole". But this is a false concept of liberation and only denounces a major ineptitude to express oneself. Art is not sterile; it performs a practical and useful function to develop the perceptibility of society as a whole. No matter how individualistic, trend setting or reforming he pretends to be, the authentic artist has the unavoidable social commitment to decipher the world, which his particular innate qualities allow him to perceive in a more accurate and meticulous manner, to transmit it to those who lack such ability, and improve their experience of life. The most fundamental characteristic of genuine art is that it escapes its creator and becomes universal. And precisely, because it manages to touch the deepest and most essential fibers of the soul of all Human Beings. Nevertheless, one of the great prides of modernism is the so-called abstract art which, on not being based on reality but rather on an "innovative" quest that goes beyond our natural perceptions, our senses fail to grasp it to translate it into meaningful emotions. This explains why, along with all of its warped variants, its presence has been fleeting and hesitant. The portraits of deformed beings, with the pretentious intention of creating implausible images where the various facets of an individual or the world are simultaneously depicted, something that is not only impossible in a human being but also abnormal for reality, are a reflection of the degradation of the spirit and of our estrangement from Nature, coupled with a sick desire to manipulate it, to destroy it as we please. The distortion of the world as a consequence of the deformity of the soul. These cartoonish images are fine as entertainment for children or people with limited mental faculties, remember the talking pigs? But for someone who seeks to expand his perception of the environment that surrounds us they're merely restrictive disfigurements. The most sarcastic thing is that despite all these ineptitudes and deficiencies, they still pretend to be considered as geniuses, owners of an ultrahuman sensibility, beyond the reach of everyone else. The key to "interpreting" their "great works" is in the outrageous prices at which they're sold. Just crystal clear. Idealism itself must be grounded in reality to be viable. What good is the idiotic longing to be invisible or to be eternal?

Beyond words is the most universal and expressive of all languages: Music; which at its most sublime level speaks directly to the soul, without going through the mind. It always leaves me enraptured to confirm the reassuring effect that a few rhythmic pats on the chest or back have on my little son. When his sleep becomes unquiet, this simple affectionate gesture restores his calm. The reason is very simple: Percussions belong to the most natural and primitive rhythms, and they're one of the first sounds we hear. The charm emanates from a pleasant memory, distant and nebulous remembrances lost in our subconscious that make us relive that period of our sojourn in our mother's womb, which provided us with food, warmth, peace…Where the rhythmic beating of our mother's heart filled all of our universe. That's why the music where percussions set the tone, especially when its beating gets close to that of cardiac frequency, has such a gratifying impression on our mood; like the African rhythms, so archaic, and yet so striking. It's just liked the reflex to curl up in a fetal position to protect ourselves. They simply transport us to the early stages of our existence; happy times when all of our vital and affective needs were satisfied.

This is the starting point. Nevertheless, as human beings, we have a duty to improve, not to remain at such a basic level. Just as the intellect must be broadened, the human soul must also be expanded to increase its emotional potential. Music sharpens the senses turning them more and more refined, widening the boundaries of our sensibility to perceive aspects of our surroundings that, at first, slip away without us noticing them. Its limits are only the brain's innate ability to soar to higher levels, or our ineptitude to find the mechanisms to fully develop such ability. Unfortunately, given the huge influence it has on us, music has been manipulated into a weapon of domestication that stuns and blocks the senses. Such is the case of so-called pop music, with its monotonous and repetitive rhythms that imprison the Being and render the mind stupid. The question is limited to a commercial gain, if it makes money, it's a fantastic work; hence its success is only evaluated by its popularity, that is, by the number of imbeciles they manage to dupe into buying it; you know, the platinum prize is awarded for the number of records sold! At no time are the originality of the composition, its harmonic complexity, or at least the interpretative attributes of the alleged artist assessed. And there they are, the heavy metal bands, whose supposed music is nothing more than a string of strident noises that obfuscate the mind and dull the senses, deteriorating our perception, so much so that in order to "enjoy it", it's necessary to be stupefied under the effects of some drug. Racket, debauchery, the need to take refuge in mental derangement are signs of a dead soul. There is no happiness with fuss.

One of the crucial factors that restricts the reach of these types of music is the presence of the human voice. Words are processed in the mind, causing the piece of music to get stuck in it, preventing it from flowing into the soul for engaging in a dialog. Notable exceptions are choral music and some glorious operas in which the human voice reaches tonalities indistinguishable from those of musical instruments. The same thing occurs with poetry, whose "musicality" determines its potential to link to our spirit. In contrast, the so-called "classical" music, inspired by Nature, and of which one of its main attributes is the absence of the human voice, spontaneously transcends to the soul, liberating it, stimulating its creative zones; it launches it to wander through the sublime, awakening unknown emotions. It's like learning a new language that allows us to interpret the reality that envelops us in a more profound and significant way. There are few moments as grandiose as those when the percussions make way for the echoes of almost celestial trumpets, to lead us to a spiritual fugue to the confines of sidereal space. There is a very obvious and simple way to evaluate the excellence and relevance of music: If it incites you to move your body, to dance, it's just that it has gotten stuck in your mind, trapping it; and it won't take you beyond a corporeal experience. Even horses like to dance! If, on the contrary, it leaves you static, absorbed, it's because it has enraptured the soul, which, entranced, escapes to enter into communion with the Cosmos.

Just as music feeds the soul, study, culture, experience, expand and free the mind. The objective must be to achieve the full development of both to complete our growth as humans. Hence the enormous importance of education. For centuries it was considered a privilege to which few had access. Today, sadly, it has not only been devalued, but has become a mechanism of indoctrination. Even millionaires and merchants vociferate labelling it useless, and urge the student to rather concentrate on activities that generate "riches". It's terrifying to confirm that after more than twenty years of school education, complexes and prejudices cannot be overcome. It's a lie that a college graduate be a cultured person. His time at the university only serves to indoctrinate him and transform him into a slave to a society immersed in consumerism. His desires go no further than gaining money to amass superfluous material goods. Even worse, upon completing his studies the person ends up pigeonholed. Lawyers, physicians, engineers, whatever, they no longer aspire to more, they are left socially stereotyped, and that's as far as they go. As if man could be programmed like a robot to perform a single function. The point is that being cultured doesn't mean to know a whole lot of useless things, but knowing what helps you to set yourself free. Culture is the means to increase the sensibility of the soul and the acuity of the intellect.

But the sophisticated techniques of manipulation for commercial purposes have wreaked true havoc. We founder in a regression that not only has made us clumsier, but we have also lost aptitudes and instincts. In the advance party goes television, closely followed by fantasy novels and films, spreading distorted ideas; with some "creators" with such a grotesque and sick mentality that, frankly, it's nauseating. Even those that are said to be biographical are fictitious, they twist the facts to conform to the ideology that they're intending to inculcate, they're destined to tame. If you don't see or read them, rest assured that you're not missing anything. And you're not going to spend the rest of your life learning about the "fabulous" life of others instead of living your own; above all when they're just a bunch of deceitful imbeciles that the media wants to present them to you as if they were special beings, gifted with unattainable attributes. The human being has too many dreams and aspirations to deal with, and there is no time to waste. Do not allow them to subjugate you with impunity. It's not the same to guide and to orient to find the way than plying us with propaganda to domesticate us. Read reportages, dissertations, documentaries that allow you to learn about geography, history, diverse cultures. Place yourself in the Universe! Don't forget that reality far surpasses fantasy.

Let's go to schools and universities. Anyone who has had the school experience has noticed that not everyone is qualified to be a student, let alone a university students The institutions are full of mediocre students incapable of handling subjects that involve even the most basic use of the intellect. It's these "dunces" who wind up in the less demanding faculties such as the one of political sciences. Unfortunately, they are the ones who will end up being the politicians who occupy the command positions in the governments. And then we wonder why we're doing so badly. A dumbass, even if he studies at the best university on the planet, will never stop being a dumbass. To be able to improve, it's crucial to implement an admission system that strictly selects who should access higher education on the basis of his innate intellectual merits, to make the most of resources and to ensure a pool of capable professionals. On the other hand, for the proper functioning and stability of a society it's also necessary to have good masons, electricians, carpenters and many other indispensable trades, and there are people who were born for that; there is nothing denigrating about this. You just have to assure them fair wages that give them a decent quality of life; we must all contribute to the general welfare. Sadly, the group in power is well aware of the Machiavellian motto "Divide and conquer", and it provokes confrontations between the different social strata to be able to manipulate and use them to satisfy its unrestrained ambition. Just as beauty has been idolized, a worrisome current trend of domestication has idealized and extolled youth as if it were a permanent condition, a stage that belongs exclusively to them. That a young person is never going to grow old! Due to their inexperience and impulsiveness, they are easy prey for advertising, and a whole fashion and a way of life have been created for them, which they must accept without questioning. Dazzled, they forget that it's only an ephemeral period that they're going to leave behind sooner than they imagine. But they almost convince them that adults are a different species. This deception has caused severe intergenerational conflicts that seriously affect social coexistence. Contrary to past cultures in which the elderly was respected and valued as a source of wisdom, today they are a hindrance that must be discarded; first of all because their prudent perception of reality makes them very bad consumers. But, in the majority of cases, the fact of growing old not only highlights the success of having managed to better adapt oneself to survive more years, but also of achieving the intellectual and emotional maturity that leads to fully understand and enjoy life, far from consumerism and materialism.

Another of the great tools of domination is to resort to the mental alienation of fanaticism. Watching sports has become a resource to fill our dead time, offering us fleeting and frivolous emotions with the "wonderful" advantage that we do not require to make any effort; to enjoy them we can be lying down and eating like pigs. And who cares if it's just a trickery that is producing exorbitant earnings for a gang of crooks who take advantage of our stupidity. Have you ever pondered, for even a moment, what real sense does it make to be watching a bunch of idiots running around for a small ball, or swimming laps in a pool to demonstrate who is better? What a ghastly extreme of imbecility! The best these paper heroes can aspire to is wasting their time bent on winning a gold medal, fame or money to satisfy their ego. But, being admired by a horde of brainless people, who ceaselessly repeat that we're special, is not going to satiate our vanity. In the end, when reality prevails, we realize the senselessness of those hollow and trivial values. Competing against the others is an absurdity, the foe to vanquish, the most nefarious, is you yourself, your apathy, your fears, your complexes; there's no way to deceive ourselves. We cannot escape from our mediocrity, no matter what mask we wear in front of the others.

In the latest episode of our stubborn struggle to conceive the most inconceivable aberrations to satisfy our exacerbated hyper humanism, we invented the deranged craze for the, bombastically called, "emotional support" animals. Dogs, cats and the rest, destined to fill the vacuous existence of individuals incapable of finding an authentic meaning in life. Unable to provide for their own subsistence, as Nature demands, these animals are noxious and useless for the planet. Even worse, they are a pretext to promote imbecility. We have been convinced that this propensity reflects the refinement of the goodness and commiseration that characterize our avant-garde civilization. Even in countries that go further beyond avant-gardism, they have come to the extreme of wanting to enshrine the rights of these animals in the constitution! But it turns out that NO! When we analyze the symbiotic relationship that ancient peoples have developed with animals, which help carrying out useful and productive activities, feeding themselves naturally without having to destroy the environment, we see what a degree of perversion we have reached. Most seriously, this tendency is born from the advertising manipulation by companies that produce pet food, to increase their sales. Once again, to make money at any cost. With cute commercials where funny and playful puppies appear as part of our family, they have managed to captivate our ostentatious sentimentality. But these companies are the main culprits of the deforestation of jungles and forests to turn them into pasture land where to breed cheap cattle to make their products. Have you seen the photos of the jungles devastated by fire, where a multitude of bodies of wild animals lie scorched? Species brought to the brink of extinction so that our pets can have a "balanced diet" and grow healthy. And even if we want to close our eyes and feign dementia, we're directly responsible for this massacre and destruction. Just like drug addicts are direct culprits of the violence and carnages caused by drug trafficking.

Degeneration has reached such disgusting limits that already there are even psychologists for parrots! Imprisoning and corrupting animals is not creating a bond with Nature, it's promoting its deterioration. Let's have the courage to face the challenges of going out to contemplate them enjoying their world, in freedom.

It was supposed that progress, technological advance, would liberate us from routine, dangerous, or brutalizing activities, and it would give us more free time to devote to cultivating the soul and expanding the intellect, thereby fostering individual and social development. But in a society where futile individuals, without initiative, without anything to improve, abound, free time is lost time. The sole thing it gave rise to was idleness, the seed of all vices. The mediocre man drowns in boredom; not knowing what to do with freedom, he wastes it on becoming even more stupid. What would his life be if there were no "blessed social networks" or television to get away? He would simply have to put up with himself; with his hollow mind and his dead soul. Incapable of creating ideas, all he can do is to imitate the others. From here emerged fashion, beauty parlors, gyms, the illustrious bodybuilders... So many banalities created by frivolous people to squander life. A creative person lacks in time to complete his projects. Being a rational and meditative creature, the Human Being needs solitude, peace and silence to find inspiration and deploy his creativity; this is just what the experience of immersing ourselves in the natural world affords us, where our senses get activated, sharpening our perception, liberating us. Solitude has the attribute of facing us with our conscience; that's why a thinking being seeks it to have a space for introspection; the pusillanimous one, on the contrary, is afraid of it and doesn't know what to do with it because it confronts him with his inner void. Since the dawn of the sciences devoted to the study of man, the idea that the human being is a social being was forged; shortly after this notion was distorted, insisting on the folly that humans have the unavoidable necessity of living in a group. But there is an abyss between being a social being and requiring to belong to a herd, losing all consciousness of individuality. Suffice it to consider an atrocious historical event to disprove such a concept: The man working alone managed to deduce the very essence of matter, the elemental structure of the Cosmos; by comparison, the man working in team, of which so much bragging is made in the "advanced" countries, used this knowledge to build the atomic bomb, the most infamous, perverse and ignominious weapon ever conceived. The human adventure is in essence a solitary experience; to wander among the crowd searching for a place for oneself that, simply, does not exist. The naïf who does not realize it as soon as possible, and understands that, despite everything, it's a unique opportunity worth taking advantage of, is condemned to an existence of frustrations and bitterness. One of the most relevant experiences that solitude gives us, when we have the courage to overcome the uncertainty and risks of exploring the world, is the chance to feel the rapture of discovery.

Spurred on by a string of pseudo experts, who no one knows how, what or who made them "experts", we boast that we're superior beings because we have the ability to modify the environment and "to dominate" the other beings that dwell in it. But it's a lie! In actual fact, we do not dominate, we destroy. Science has become our great pride, and we almost consider it a goddess to whom we thank for the Artifiture in which we live. We fantasize that our modernity by itself has made us evolve and become more intelligent and spiritual, owners of a unique ultra-sensibility, never seen on the globe. Nonetheless, the irreverent reality, once again, contradicts us. The intellectual profoundness and the clarity of discernment of Plato or Aristotle thousands of years ago, are incomparable even today. Totally out of its natural milieu our understanding has been obfuscated. Entire generations were born and raised imprisoned between plastic and cement; so much so that they have never even seen a goat or a hen in real life. On the other hand, it's indispensable to individualize because generalizations tend to be incorrect. Scientific and technical breakthroughs have been achieved by a fistful of brilliant individuals; the rest is just a manipulable mob, a useless burden, without the slightest idea of how or what has been attained; although our boastfulness pretends to make us part of such achievements. The blessed Industrial Revolution, which we consider quite a milestone in our civilization, besides achieving the "glorious" women's liberation, it generated a severe city versus country conflict. The "rough" peasant, exiled from the countryside due to the mechanization of agricultural labor, and the artisan, ruined by his impossibility to compete against the factories, were forced to take refuge in the city, where they ended up forming the proletariat, the working class at the service of the "refined" urban bourgeoisie, which imposed customs and values that exalted its virtues, and belittled the economic and social "inferiority" of the "plebs", to marginalize them and get hold of power. Over the years, living in the city was considered a symbol of prestige, at the same time that life in the rural areas was denigrated, considering their inhabitants as ignorant, retrograde and lacking in initiative. This conditioned in the new generations of the villages a desire to emigrate to enjoy all the wonderful advantages and opportunities that large metropolises offered and to integrate themselves into modernity. But the most serious consequence was that the creation of banal and superfluous occupations and jobs was fostered, which gave room to mediocre and useless people, promoting their proliferation. You know, the more customers, the more profit. Currently, this unsustainable tendency has reached colossal proportions, giving rise to monstrous megacities that not only devastate natural resources and pollute the environment, but also dehumanize their inhabitants. It's from this putrefaction that so many parasites have arisen, so many mentally sick people who pack out the world, and who have made them their refuge, where all perversion is valid to escape from the inner emptiness. In little more than a century, our hubris and ambition have brought the earth to the brink of disaster. Our pompous consumerist and comfort-loving society, fond of waste and the ridiculous hyper humanism that allows the survival of inept people, is out of all vital cycle and is completely opposed to natural laws. We have simply created a civilization that IS NOT VIABLE on the planet. The much touted "progress" is a "mortal cycle" where what matters the least is fostering our evolution as humans. It's limited to a frenzied technological transformation that requires malleable individuals, to exploit them as consumerist slaves and to achieve enrichment to pathological degrees of a few. Our arrogance does not allow us to understand that in order to learn from Nature we must ask those who live in Nature, the indigenous peoples who know and follow its laws, not the "know-it-all" scientists who live outside of it. To evolve is to improve, and the goal is to reach the point of natural equilibrium where it's no longer required to keep "advancing". Nature teaches it to us bluntly; some reptiles, such as the crocodile, and certain insects have managed to integrate themselves in such a perfect way to their milieu that they have not suffered alterations in their body structure for millions of years. There are also human groups that over the millennia have kept a way of life that is completely in harmony with their environment, in an admirable symbiotic relationship. This is the pinnacle of evolutionary adaptation. But the fact that we can learn a lot from these peoples, to whom we persist in considering wild and primitive, even outdated, is inadmissible to our pretentious space age mentality. pursuit of new horizons thing about the tragicomedy is that, in the end, it's most likely that they be the only ones who survive.

And speaking of space; being on the verge of annihilating the earth and under the pretext of saving ourselves from a potential cosmic cataclysm, we have engaged in a senseless race to explore new frontiers, in quest of other habitable planets that we can destroy to satisfy our whims. You know, the important thing is that we survive, it doesn't matter if, like a plague, we have to pollute and devastate the entire universe. We refuse to take cognizance that eventually the Universe itself is going to die to start a new cycle; no matter how much we flee like cowards, destiny will catch up with us. By what miraculous intercession, by what supra natural merits do we pretend that we deserve to be eternal? We've reached the climax of imbecility. For now, much like the immensity of the sea that seemed endless, we have filled the space arounds us with garbage to wage war and obtain the largest possible economic benefit. But again, we bump into the real world. When we realize the formidable barrier that the vastness of Cosmos constitutes, the impracticability of these harebrained projects of conquest, with the means of transport that modern science has managed to envisage, becomes immediately evident. Nevertheless, the heroic astronauts already brag about their grandiose sacrifice in the pursuit of new horizons. The most ironic thing is that the underestimated ancient civilizations and their millenary wisdom could teach us a far simpler method to be able to travel through space: The interstellar portals. However, and as always, pedantry and disdain do not allow us to conceive that these archaic cultures could know something that be useful to us. For the sake of scientific precision, the "experts" stubbornly object to and dismiss the ancestral knowledge in advance, no matter how obvious it be. It's been already a long time since Einstein intuited them and showed us a path to follow; now it's a matter of taking a step further, putting aside complexes and prejudices, and focusing our efforts on discovering how they are activated, in order to gain access to them. We cannot continue to fill the space with shit, with impunity. The gateway to the stars is here, on earth.

Nobody is against true progress; general progress as a product of the intellect and sensibility of a Human Being, based on the guidelines and limits imposed by the natural framework, and not on the economic and military interests of pigs with a twisted concept of the world. To solve the problem in depth, it's urgent to establish mechanisms to eliminate these monsters full of evil. If we want to evolve as a species, it's indispensable to seek the benefit of all the inhabitants of the planet, to conceive ourselves as humanity, to adopt drastic measures to direct our advance, to safeguard the wellbeing of the earth as our common home. We cannot disregard reality. It must be understood that our future is not in technology, but in Nature. It's not about making more sophisticated and efficient vehicles to provide us with comforts, it's about man walking again; about building cities on a human scale and strictly controlling population growth to respect the ecosystems that surround us. No woman must have children before turning thirty-three, an age perfectly within the ideal range for conception, and never more than two. Reproductive conditions have enormously changed with the development of medicine. The objective of an authentic science should be to contribute to improve our quality of life leaving out commercial considerations, and with a strict focus on anticipating the damages that its "great advances" could cause. Naturalism is simply going back to our roots, revaluing the truly transcendental things. We have been led to believe that we'll come to an end where we'll live "happily ever after", as in fairy tales. This is a stupidity. Life is a constant struggle full of challenges, that is exactly what makes it worth living! If something characterizes the Universe, it's continuous change, a dynamic existence where the only stable thing is instability. Routine kills creativity and dulls thinking; we're the living example. For primitive man each day was different, a new opportunity to learn, to experiment, to die; it was what made him evolve. We must fill ourselves with emotions, create dreams, set goals that bring us closer to the sublime. The most terrible thing is that you put up barriers for yourself or cut your wings. Why are we going to respect the rules and morals of a sick civilization that is devastating the planet? They want to make us fall into a trap to tame us. Our freedom only depends on us. Jump monkey, jump, or they get you caged!

CHAPTER VI

MY SELF, MY OTHER SELF AND MY ALL TINY SELFISH SELF

The Burden of Obscurity

She could have been Creole. I never knew it. Her light-colored eyes, transparent as honey, her complexion so fair, her subtly golden braids. My grandfather, quite the opposite. Even if he was not a Tente en el Aire (Stay in the Air) or a Saltapatrás (Jump Backwards), he was very swarthy; black his eyes, and straight the hair. Certainly not a Mulatto, but a Mestizo with strong indigenous blood. With what a pleasure I remember those stories of his childhood, when he accompanied his parents to go to the City of México in small canoes, crossing the majestic lake. In the ancient village still exists a monument that marks the site to where the water reached. There was the pier from which Cortez set off to conquer the great Tenochtitlán. Three centuries of mishmash followed; the Spanish invaders had no qualms about mixing with the local indigenous

75

women, and upon arrival of black slaves, endless racial combinations were originated. When other Europeans, Chinese, Arabs and the others showed up, and added themselves to the jumble, that turned into a veritable hodgepodge. Each resulting group received a specific name, but over the years they became so numerous that appellatives were lacking, and it was necessary to resort to ingenuity. Thus, were born the Lobo Tornatrás (Wolf going back), the Alli te Estás (There you Stay), the No te Entiendo I don't understand you, and many more. Nevertheless, these castes or social classes didn't constitute a rigid and strict classification of the community, rather than a racial division, they were based on economic parameters, in fact, the next generation could change caste if they married someone from a different group or if their financial position improved. In time, out of this centenarian melting pot a race of bronze emerged.

Things were quite different much further north, where a group of pilgrims bringing on their backs a heavy burden of religious prejudices, also came to claim by force a land that was not theirs. But, in addition, their puritanical scruples were insurmountable and didn't allow them to merge with the indigenous groups that inhabited the region; instead, they practically exterminated them. They betrayed their good faith by dispossessing them of their villages, murdering or enslaving their children and women in unspeakable crimes against humanity. The passing of centuries turns blurry such fateful calamities and fades our indignation. But, to give us a more precise and current idea, suffice it to imagine that someone unexpectedly comes to seize our house, evicting us violently, and killing our children, just because he has the power to satisfy his ambition. Throughout the continent, horrendous massacres, humiliations, pillages and atrocities took place, upon which the prosperity and development of the old world were founded, and in front of which the infamies of the world wars pale. The conquest of América was one of the most aberrant and bloody episodes in the history of mankind. But today, who remembers it? They were just a bunch of Indians!

And we come to the most controversial topic of this book, where reality becomes brutally present. In analyzing past evidence and testimonies, it's very patent how human society, by observing animal societies and based on a deep intuition emanating from the most elemental common sense, discerned that there were also palpable intrinsic differences among its members, perhaps subject to destiny or heavenly designs. This conditioned a social behavior that tended to classify its members according to their innate qualities or defects. In fact, it was what in remote times gave rise to surnames. Thus, the skills for some trade or the place of birth, or also the distinctive traits of the temperament of the people, were taken into account. We've all heard, for instance, the last names Shoemaker, Armstrong or Good. In rural communities, still attached to natural guidelines, people continue to differentiate the slackers, the hard workers, the idiots and others. And they not only call them as such, they treat them as such! From here arose countless sayings that summarized the wisdom acquired over time and that clearly identified the attributes of each individual: Like father, like son; as the twig is bent, so grows the tree; you cannot make a silk purse out of a sow's ear. And this is all the more remarkable because such sayings have astonishing equivalents in varied cultures around the world, even though some of them never had contact with each other. Thus, social strata have naturally existed since forever; they instinctively perceived the reality: WE ARE NOT ALL EQUAL. The problem arose when this classification deviated from the only valid natural parameters: Mental and spiritual capabilities. As artificial variables without any real foundation, born of prejudices, complexes and the abuse of power were used as elements of judgement, an unacceptable discrimination was originated. Social classes appeared whose justification was the place of origin, religion, language. At present, with our instincts dulled, we've gone to the other extreme; we want to pretend that we're all equal and that everyone must have the same rights.

But Nature has already determined the talent of each person, and established a natural order where each one plays a certain role. There is sufficient evidence throughout history to be able to classify people. Furthermore, these differences are of paramount importance because they serve to give viability to society, enabling, in mutual cooperation, the different tasks that are necessary for its survival to be carried out. Human society is a living being, just like the human body itself, which needs lungs, kidneys, heart, to perform, each one, a specific function that contributes to the benefit of the organism as a whole. It's a matter of observing the natural world, as of yore; the animals that live in society show us the way. Every human group needs a minimum of social organization. Hierarchical order serves as moral support to a community; that's why when its leaders are corrupt or wicked, they lose all authority and societies collapse. Not everyone can be captain, there must be sailors, cooks, janitors… and they are all important! Else, the ship cannot sail.

Let's go back to definitions, and already put on track, let's move on to classifications. In conclusion: According to our innate faculties in the intellectual and spiritual fields, we'll reach a certain rank in the social scale which, at the same time, will determine our task. These parameters allow us to quite clearly differentiate the following strata:

1- The Human Being. This is the highest level we can aspire to as a species. The serious thing is that he's on the verge of extinction; they are very scarce and their number continues to decline dramatically. He's characterized by having a conception of existence that goes beyond simple survival. Given his peculiar scale of values, he understands that his life, in itself, is not that essential and valuable, and he is capable of dying for an ideal. He realizes with absolute clarity his place in Nature, which demands a minimum of stoicism, what implies corporeal sacrifice; the human body is designed to make efforts, to work physically. Even though he needs independence, he has a profound social consciousness and seeks the general welfare. Elemental logic, living in a healthy society favors his own health. His greatest desires are: To comprehend and experience the wonderful adventure of his fleeting passage on earth, and to reach the intellectual and spiritual evolution that leads him to authentic freedom, which inexorably demands of our five senses. The value of life as a human is determined by the capability to be useful and to integrate oneself into the perennial cycle of the Cosmos.

2- The Person. It's the second largest group in society. They have a certain intellectual and spiritual level, but they don't manage to escape the guidelines established by advertising manipulation, which alienate them and make them lose their liberty. They are, therefore, the main factor that gives life and maintains our pathological civilization. The majority are good and honest individuals, but with very limited aspirations. Corporeal issues are of utmost importance and they settle for a pragmatic life. Among their essential goals are to achieve the security and peace of routine. The worst in this category is the mediocre one, who constitutes a good part of it and who is saved by a single step from falling to the lower rung. He's very easy to identify: He only has the capacity to focus on himself; he lives cloistered in his own little world from which it's unimaginable for him to leave. He loves to follow fashion trends. He considers his feelings and well-being to be the most important things, and he takes for granted that the world and things exist solely to satisfy his needs; it couldn't be otherwise, being a direct descendant of deities, he deserves it! In his myopic perspective there is nothing but the present, it has always been there; the efforts of all previous generations, the past and the others, do not count. How does it affect me? What does it matter to me? What do I get for me? The typical all tiny me-me, center of the universe, who in his delusions of grandeur imagines that, if he is not happy, the earth will stop turning and the sun will stop burning.

3- The Animals. They form the bulk of the population. If you prefer you can call them The Beasts, or affectionately The Sweety Brutes, it's the same. Their main characteristic is that they live the life of the *"decease"*, Dine, Crap and Screw. As long as this is not lacking, they are satisfied and "happy". They are incapable of having initiative to create dreams and set goals. From birth they bring limitations and deficiencies, they go no further than performing instinctive functions; their soul is dead and their mind does not manage to express by itself. They need to be led in hordes to feel safe. You must show them the way, tell them what they need, what they have to think, what they have to feel. Their life goals are limited to consumerism and killing time; thus, their great allies are television, the cell phone, the gym or any other stupidity that fills their inner void. They are the main target of advertising aimed at homogenizing and massifying, as if it were a virtue to live crowded like cattle. Therefore, it's very easy to differentiate the individuals of this group, the closer their mental level is to that of animals, the more need they have to belong to a flock. Have you noticed the behavior of the multitudes that fill the stadiums? Nonetheless, the best ones of this group are useful beings as they carry out activities relevant to social welfare, and while they're secondary, this in no way is undeserving, suffice it to consider the humble and silent work that a good plumber performs, liberating mankind of all of its shit. At the bottom of this stratum are the dumbasses: Banal, docile, indolent individuals, totally comparable to an animal. And it's just that being a dumbass, what ordinary people call a dumbass, is a true tragedy. And you know, there is nothing worse than a dumbass with initiative.

4- The Hapless Ones. These are the forgotten of god; those who, if a minimum of celestial compassion existed, should not even come into the world. The majority is born with irremediable physical or mental defects that will impede them from living in plenitude. At times their condition is the result of illness or an accident at a later stage in life. The most unfortunates can barely be compared to a vegetable. They don't have the capability to survive in Nature. By themselves they would die in the short term, if they are lucky; otherwise, they are condemned to a wretched and unhappy life. It's against them that the current hyper humanism shows no mercy. From the intoxicated perspective of an unbridled and debased goodness, they claim that life must be preserved for life itself, without taking into account the quality of life. This is very easy when you're not the one who is bedridden for life or the one who cannot have a normal social relationship. Or when you're not the one who carries the emotional and economic burden of having to live with someone with these limitations. All those super merciful people should be forced to take charge of their care and support, to confront them with reality to see how compassionate they really are. In our ailing pseudo humanism, we've reached the extreme of considering that it's more humane to deceive hope, even if that increases suffering, by prolonging a horrendous and painful agony, and affectively and financially exhausting families, instead of allowing a dignified death by simply accepting the natural laws. We rant against euthanasia, even if the patient himself demands it as the sole escape from his condition, and yet we permit the grotesque enrichment of health merchants at the expense of artificially prolonging the miserable existence of terminally ill patients. What a filth of morals we have created!

5- The Sacks of Shit. Their name says it all. They're hollow beings whose body is just a container, a sack replete with crap. They're born with a dead soul, and what little mind they have is barely enough to generate evil ideas. Although they constitute a small part of society, they're the most noxious and wicked. Frivolous and selfish, unable to love or create true dreams and ideals, their insatiable avarice plunges them into materialism without ever finding spiritual peace. Vain power, money, comforts, are their only objectives in life, it doesn't matter if to achieve them, they have to harm the others. They need the servility and admiration of other imbeciles to feel that they're worth something, to counter their complexes and prejudices, and to silence the consciousness of their own inferiority. Their most "illustrious" exponents are malefactors, corrupt politicians and quite a lot of moneyed people. Balzac already said it: "Behind every great wealth lies a great crime". The great advantage is that it's very easy to identify them; the vast majority are impeccably dressed in a gleaming suit and a useless and idiotic tie around the neck, which makes them feel like the epitome of elegance. Oh! And many of them love to play golf. These distinguished uniformed people have caused the most horrendous and cruel calamities mankind has ever known.

Let's digress a bit to address a crucial question. With so many eminent psychologists interpreting and reinventing reality at their whim, out of ignorance, the concept that delinquents are made, not born, has been taken as true; to justify themselves, they have produced an endless string of culprits. This has served as a pretext for the compassionate defenders of the distorted human rights and the avant-garde hyper humans **to** argue that they're victims of their environment, their poverty, their disintegrated families. But a simple actual fact and the most elementary common sense, suffice to disprove all these stupidities of a pseudo-science that needs to have proof of the obvious. If these factors were the real cause of wickedness, there wouldn't be a single rich individual, from a good family, who were evil; and not a single poor person without a family, who were good. History is full of stories of humble people, even orphans, who in terrible times managed to overcome all adversities to be useful to society. Wickedness, that perverse tendency to harm the others is brought from birth. The delinquent IS BORN, not made. Just the same as a schizophrenic or a depraved person who likes to be fucking hens, the criminal has a congenital cerebral disorder. But here a very important factor is added: In the vast majority of the brains of malefactors a palpable, REAL anatomic defect has been found, which determines their antisocial behavior. In other words, he's a being with anatomical, physiological and even genetic flaws and deficiencies that predispose him to a malevolent conduct. It's a similar case, but at the opposite end, to that of geniuses, who are already born with that faculty! And there's no way to teach anyone to be a genius, be it a rich, poor or blue-blooded person, although, in our foolish and corrupted logic, today we intend to make them by hammer blows. And yes, reality is overwhelming and undeniable, there are not only second-class men and women, but even of fourth and fifth rate, who do not have, and will NEVER reach, the human level. That's why the efforts and the squandering of resources to "rehabilitate" criminals are in vain. It's stupid to think that they're going to reform with the simple threat that, if they keep on beheading people, Satan is going to take them to hell!

The myth of human rights has only served to allow mediocre, inept and pusillanimous people to survive, seriously affecting society. It's of vital urgency to make a Universal Declaration of Human Duties where the requirements that must be fulfilled in order to be considered as a Human Being are clearly stated. And that is because, as in all health issues, the best remedy is prevention. Just the same as what occurs in the human body, these useless parasites weaken society and perform no productive role to offset the benefits they derive from living off the efforts of others. The key point is to prevent them from occupying command positions where they can exert their negative influence, since they're willing to do anything to achieve it. They were born to be flunkies, and up to there they must get! There are few things worse than a flunky pretending to be a boss. The question is as simple as taking care of a garden. In order for the lawn, the flowers and fruits to be able to germinate, it's necessary to uproot, incessantly, the weeds so that they do not invade and destroy it, there is no way to reform nor to be lenient about them. Pruning just the leaves is futile, the solution involves a constant and thorough work. Death penalty is indispensable, NOT AS A DETERRENCE METHOD, but to exterminate pests! The fight against wickedness is something permanent. Perverse people will continue to be born and it's necessary to implement mechanisms to detect and eradicate them as soon as possible, before they begin to harm society, or the consequences will be regrettable and even irremediable. A very illustrative example: Gang members. There is nothing more repulsive and cowardly than a being who is capable of assaulting a defenseless person with premeditation, treachery and advantage. This is not a juvenile prank, it's a warped and wicked mind. Every society has the obligation to get rid of them without delay. Perpetrators of serious crimes must be summarily executed, regardless of their age, there is no other option. It's a lie they can be mended. This is about liberating society, and in passing the poor planet, from so many filthy pigs. Those who commit minor crimes can be given an opportunity to rectify, punishing them with forced labors to compensate a bit for the harm they've done, which also serves to discharge their energy and not to be idle in a cell. Let's not forget that idleness is the beginning of all vices. Prisons must be eliminated; all the more so now that they've become a lucrative business. They correct nothing; they're just a source of corruption and true operation and recruitment centers of the criminal groups. It's unacceptable that, in addition to having to suffer the damage they cause, we must also bear the economic burden of maintaining them, wasting resources that would avail much better to support healthy people with more promising future expectations. That should be the role of god: To extirpate weeds. But the sucker likes to play the asshole, and he has sunk humanity into chaos. Given his flagrant omission, it's up to us to take responsibility for creating legal procedures to fight them and prevent their propagation. A criminal is NOT a Human Being. If you consider that a kidnapper and murderer is the same as Pasteur or Madame Curie, the one who is wrong and sick is you. Period! If that were my concept of the Human Being, I would have thrown myself off the highest bridge of my village long ago.

Let's focus on another very serious problem that has caused incommensurable afflictions to mankind. The adaptation to the environment entails physical and physiological transformations to withstand the various climatic conditions created by geography. This gave rise to races, which ended up living in the most suitable places according to their corporeal characteristics. The invention and improvement of means of transportation allowed the groups to move to neighboring areas, at first to trade. But the unrestrained ambition for dominance started deplorable conflicts that linger up to this day. These campaigns of conquest based on violence created the notion that brute force backed by war technology were symbols of superiority. Since then, the fundamental human components, the mind and the soul, left the equation of progress. The shocking picture of the abominable murder of Archimedes by an irate Roman soldier perfectly illustrates the idea. It's important to emphasize that the current concept of race and therefore racism appeared towards the end of the XVIII century. As we've seen, social classes or castes were determined by the financial situation, and established a pragmatic political-economic system to exploit labor force; in no way did they carry implicit racial prejudice. In fact, the laws of genetics being unknown at those distant times, the color of the skin got to be even attributed to the person's diet! Nowadays conditions have radically changed. We've reached the inconceivable extreme where people consider themselves superior just by having light skin and eyes, no matter they have an exanimate soul and a hollow mind. What an enormous stupidity!!

The justification is that it was in these communities of white people where modern civilization arose, the great advance achieved by technological development, do you remember the brilliant "Industrial

Revolution"? Logically, they close their light eyes to the havoc that this grandiose "progress" has wreaked. Their pride is having filled the earth with shit. Reality is absolutely irrefutable. The more industrialized and "advanced" a society is, the more toxic it is for the planet; among other things because it allows the survival of mediocre and imbecile people whose needs are greater and more noxious; they're the ones who give life to consumerism. One of the few sustainability studies that have been carried out yielded overwhelming results: If by magic we would suddenly manage all the inhabitants of the planet to have the same standard of living as in the "rich" countries, the earth's natural resources would be depleted in less than a decade! That's how terrifying the squandering is. Actually, the white race is biologically weaker, hence its need to modify its environment to be able to survive. The extreme case of the albino mutation lays bare indisputably the biological fragility of white skin. Ironically, the abuse of technology has made it even frailer. On the contrary, the denigrated native peoples of the earth, short, dark-skinned races, incapable of *"improving their living conditions"* by inventing fabulous technologies. Who do not have electricity, nor cars nor sophisticated artifacts; who have learned to live in balance with their milieu, taking only what is necessary; they demonstrate an astonishing capability for adaptation which is indeed a maximum degree of evolution that, in our obtuse conception of progress, we no longer even dare to dream of. As environmental degradation increases, this achievement becomes more apparent and invaluable. It's this adaptability that counts in the natural world and makes them biologically superior, as it enables them to survive. Two overwhelming examples: When the great superpowers have invaded "poor" countries with their conceited armies, super equipped with ultra-sophisticated weaponry, a troop of badly supplied "starvelings" has put them in check, and they have defeated them! And what about the indigenous communities whose malnourished sportsmen, wearing their typical attires, vanquish the lauded high-performance athletes, subject to a professional training and diet, with last generation equipment. Apart from being an adaptation to the environment, physical characteristics have nothing to do with the intellectual and spiritual development of a person. Much like in the society in general, in all racial groups there is a handful of brilliant people and a shitload of dumbasses.

We're breaking one of the most fundamental laws of Nature: Only the most capable, the best fitted, must survive. This is, precisely, why the overpopulation of the earth has become an extremely serious problem. The great hyper humanists of our time have condemned any attempt to reduce the population, considering it an attack against our own existence, since if a critical point is reached, we'll be doomed to disappear. Let's return again to reality. The most optimistic estimates suggest that in prehistoric times the population of all of Europe was about thirty-two thousand individuals divided into small groups; it took them years to come across each other! And yet today we see the results: An appalling overpopulation. We have extrapolated this obsession with "progress" to our own condition and now we want to be more human than the Human Being. But what is inhuman is not accepting death, inhuman is getting out of the natural order, inhuman is pretending that we're gods, owners of the Universe. In a world where staying alive requires great effort, we have no right to be such imbeciles. Nature demands a minimum of qualities to deserve life. Certainly, we have the right to want to live like animals, but then we cannot demand to be treated as if we were not such. And if we're finally just going to live like pigs, let's at least try not to be that noxious. It's urgent to diminish the consumption of pernicious and polluting products, starting with plastics. Biodegradable plastic does not exist, it's a vile lie. It's a very strong artificial polymer and there is not a single biological mechanism to degrade it; used as a food wrap it's extremely harmful and one of the causes of the increase in cancer. It all indicates that Nature has begun to put a limit to the "great progress of civilization". It's the moment to assess the deterioration; to reflect and act to truly evolve. Our arrogance obfuscates us; we're still sunk in obscurantism as in the Middle Ages, and the most serious and inconceivable thing is that the bonds are the same. We must challenge the inertia of an ideology completely beyond all logic and sound judgment. We can begin by allowing our mind and soul to debut. Let's respect ourselves and aspire to become Human Beings. Let's escape the obscurity!

CHAPTER VII

THE BULL OF THE GOLDEN BALLS

The Trap of Unreality

It doesn't even take idiocy away! Nor does it refine your sensibility or make you wise. Even less does it give meaning to life, on the contrary, it narrows your vision so much that you end up sunken into frivolity. Those of my generation will probably remember the photograph of a super millionaire old man, the richest man in the world at that time, if I remember correctly, dining alone at an enormous table. How tragic that, at that age, our conception of existence revolves only around money. Investing life in becoming a millionaire is the most degrading demonstration of a resounding failure as a Human Being. What good is so much effort, to end up turned into a pig? And it's just that to get rich it's not necessary to be intelligent. If you're a hard-working person and have a bit of discipline and dedication, even selling tacos you can honestly make a lot of money. Or a stroke of luck could lead you to a highly valued invention or discovery, even if it's not something brilliant. Furthermore, you can make it by cartloads, illicitly, if your cynicism, perversity and vileness permit it to you. It's a matter of knowing and doing juicy "businesses" with a corrupt ruler or becoming a criminal, they are almost the same though. What we do not understand is that not because of being a millionaire we stop being a mediocrity. Self-deification leads to extreme selfishness and the absurdity of materialism. If you don't have the slightest idea of how to live life and value what is really important, you'll never reach happiness. Money does not fill the void of the soul. In fact, if it's bought with money, it's simply something that is not worth it, momentous things are free. History shows us that opulence and vanity end up transforming us into insatiable beasts. Certainly, living in a materialistic society, economic freedom is essential as without resources, no matter how much you flip your wig, you have no independence. That's precisely what money is for, to escape consumerism. And you don't need to have heaps of it to swim in, like the duck in the silk top hat. One characteristic that assholes, mediocre ones and wicked people all have in common is their obsession with seeing life solely as a matter of accumulating wealth. Aware of their nullity, they try to escape their frustrations and complexes by surrounding themselves with trivial luxuries to persuade themselves that the world is at their feet. They need to live in fantasy because their reality is unbearable to them. Suffice it to remember the proverb of the guy who was so poor, so poor, that all he had was lots and lots of money; and a huge empty table.

In a sick civilization, with a deformed concept of progress, the notion of a healthy economy depends on the immoderate consumption of products that are not only futile, but harmful to the planet. You just have to enter one of those department stores, emblems of our great advance, where the shelves are full of superfluous and frankly useless items. But consumerism is what gives life to our society. That's why stratospheric sums are spent on advertising, increasingly subliminal, to condition our judgment. And it's so effective that, they have not only convinced us that it's normal to live as slaves, but that it's well worth being a slave to enjoy all the "modern comforts" that are offered to us, no matter that we have to mortgage the only life we have.

Let's consider the indicators that are used to assess the health of the economy of countries: Gross Domestic Product (GDP) or, worse still, the GDP per capita. These parameters only measure the market value of all goods and services produced in a given year; at no time is the quality of life or the well-being of a society taken into account. The GDP per "noggin" simply adds up all the profits obtained in the commercial activities of a country, and divides them by the number of inhabitants of the same, as if each one of them were the owner of that capital. In reality, profits go to large companies; each individual only gets a meager salary and a good licking. But, if the GDP grows, and the companies increase their income and become richer, the country goes ahead full sail. This is how we evaluate progress! The true wealth of a country is not measured by the number of magnates it generates but by the socioeconomic conditions of those who have the least. How many people of scarce resources have access to health care, to education? How much does the execrable minimum wage meet the basic needs of a family? And it's just that, in pure economics, there is no single reason why a minimum wage should be established. The only things that justify it are the voracity, the greed and the wickedness of the pseudo entrepreneurs who want all the profit for themselves. To get exorbitant earnings, totally unjustified, for the supposed effort they do. They have widely promoted the idea that entrepreneurs are highly intelligent, wise and audacious people, worthy of admiration. Truth is that honest businessmen with a real ability to manage economy and finances are the fewest; the vast majority are true criminals in disguise who have used bribes, frauds or collusion with corrupt politicians to obtain their fortunes. They even sell toxic inventions or products so that their "businesses" develop, without any consideration for health or the environment, with the endorsement of the government! Conveniently, they have fostered the belief that their mere presence, by a miraculous effect, makes the company productive and successful. The work that employees perform, their hours of effort, their commitment, even dedicating their entire lives to the company, all of this has no positive impact on the boom that it achieves. And we still have to venerate and thank them for their great contribution in creating "jobs" that do not go beyond treating people like slaves. The cynicism of these pigs has always amazed me. How can they feed their children with ill-gotten money without having any remorse? Their pettiness reaches unbelievable degrees. No matter how much they earn, the "successful entrepreneurs" are never satisfied. The reports of the annual, and even DAILY, millionaire profits of the companies are insulting. But they cannot give up a small part of this huge income to increase the salary of the employees, and help them improve their living conditions. What do they want so much money for!? These are fortunes that will not end in generations. What such an abject avarice!

Minimum wage must ensure the welfare of families, provide them with what people ask of god in the churches: Health, house, clothing and sustenance. After all, a worker with a stable existence is going to perform better. And if we do not have the capability to see them in another way, let's imagine them as cows in a barn, the better they are cared for, the more milk they will produce! In a humane and just world, a worker's salary must depend on his skills and the specific functions he carries out, and must be directly linked to the profits that a company obtains, since his work is a crucial piece to achieve such prosperity. Remove a manager and nothing happens, remove an employee from the production line and chaos breaks loose. Just that simple. It's indisputable that the mediocrity and ignorance of an individual are going to be essential factors in determining the degree of progress that he manages to achieve, but the income of the entire workforce should not be less than thirty percent of net profits; what still leaves a very good cut to the owner. And a higher tax rate for income above a certain margin is inseparable. A society with greater purchasing power would favor a more dynamic economy and generate more wealth for all. You just have to see what happens at Christmas, when everybody receives money. It's unacceptable that, despite giving his best effort, a person cannot even meet his basic needs, and must consume his life in vain, prisoner of a situation from which there is no possible escape, and which, ultimately, will lead him to sink into frustration and resentment. And yet still, we consider ourselves humans!?

This issue of the minimum wage perfectly illustrates how a government, which is supposed to be just a public servant, becomes corrupt and neglects its function of safeguarding the welfare of the people, to allow the powerful ones to oppress the busted ones. This collusion among politicians, moneyed people and religious leaders, united to expand and retain their power is what has spoiled all efforts to advance humanity. Emperors, tyrants, and even kings by divine design! Doctrines come, doctrines go and everything has been futile. We do not manage to concretize a government system that allows us to move forward. It's not just a matter of their leaders and objectives becoming perverted; the fundamental reason is that we want to establish our own rules based on what we consider correct, or, worse still, on what is convenient for us. These prospects are untenable. Our hubris pretends to ignore that the laws, first of all, as an unappealable requisite, must be founded solely on Nature, and, secondly, they must have an authentic human sense, analyzing and weighing the real circumstances.

Thus, as a result of our obfuscation and ignorance, ideological currents such as socialism and its radical variant, communism, were born. Socioeconomic systems whose false principle is the stubbornness that we are all equal, that we all have the same rights, and we all deserve the same things. From this it derives that social classes must be abolished and assets must belong to the collectivity. With this elemental structural defect, such doctrines are doomed to failure. We have many examples of the ravages that occur when that amorphous mass called "the people" ascend to power. What else can be expected when incompetent and mediocre people take command? The ominous proverb wisely warns us: Give power to an ignoramus and you'll create a monster. Have you heard of the "Reign of Terror" following the French Revolution or the "Cultural Revolution" in China? It's worth mentioning here the stupidity of the overblown "Revolutions". Not only do they disrupt social peace and welfare, in the end, they don't even solve the root problems; other pigs equally perverse or worse end up taking over the government. Dictators, potentates or monarchs, whose predatory ambition causes the problem, as a rule, find a way to get out unscathed, and in time regain their privileges. The wealthy classes always join forces to maintain control, whereas the messy crowd of wretched people is the one that suffers the devastation and massacres. The sole real way to solve the problem is getting rid of those evil beings without that much fuss, quietly, one by one. They're not going to change; their mind is, already, deranged by power. We only have to imagine what would have happened if someone would have had the balls for killing Hitler at the beginning of his political career, even at the cost of his own life.

On the other hand, capitalism is based on the concept of private property and consumption as a generator of economic wealth. This means that, depending on the capabilities and effort of each person, a certain level of quality of life will be achieved. Government must intervene to a minimum and market forces will set the trend in consumption, and hence profits. According to the theory, as welfare conditions improve for the individuals at the top of the social pyramid, this benefit should permeate downward to the less favored classes. But it's a lie. In actual fact, wealth is not reached by the most hardworking and capable people, but by the corrupt ones and the hustlers; and their unrestrained ambition monopolizes the wealth generated and prevents the benefits from spreading to the entire population. And it's just that the system, intrinsically, is not conceived to promote the general social well-being, it needs inequality to be able to function; nevertheless, unbridled greed has caused a huge chasm that reaches shameful extremes. But the defense of ideologies, values or dignities is not included in the catalog of priorities of this doctrine; money is everything, doing business, even if it's shady, to earn as much as you can, fooling the greatest number possible of assholes. Therefore, the miserly wages destined to enslave, since only with slaves can the system survive. What they least intend is people to progress economically, because poverty is the best tool of subjugation. To that is added, leaving out all consideration of market forces and legal practices, unhealthy advertising to encourage immoderate consumption, irrational waste, and monopolies that want to hog it all; destroying with impunity the family effort of many generations. Industrial homogenization is precisely one of the most brutal attacks against human creativity. It's the opposite of the artisan work that gave sustenance and independence to countless talents. Does Stradivarius, Limoges, Baccarat tell you something? All the fascination of the diversity of the world lost to the sake of standardization at all costs to allow the survival of mediocrity and stupidity. With a materialistic goal as foundation and objective of life, based on the obsessive modernization and robotization of production, spurred on by greed and a morbid perversity, the task of achieving social advancement with this system is unfeasible. We're the civilization of wastefulness where everything is discardable, even human life. And what to say about the pollution and squandering of natural resources produced by the "blessed progress". Science and technology must be conceived as auxiliary tools to situate us in the real world and help us to fulfill a useful function on earth, nothing more. Who granted them the right to destroy Nature to satisfy their avarice? How did we get to such a mind-boggling derangement? How difficult it is to awaken consciousness when there are so many interests that seek to extinguish it.

Let's now analyze our latest "modernist" experiment. A widespread achievement in the West that bring us great complacency and boastfulness as a vanguard society: Democracy; which seeks to limit the powers of the government and grant more power to citizens. This demands people to be responsible, prepared, committed and participative. Right from the outset, we already encountered a colossal obstacle. Once again, the importance of knowing how to choose in order to have the right to choose. Even more so, given the scenario of a society largely formed by ignorant, mediocre and apathetic people, the fact that rulers are elected by the opinion of the majority, "because the majority is always right!", implies an inherent, fatal flaw that, in principle, predestines such an illusory project to failure. This was demonstrated in the very cradle of this current of political management: Athens. When the anonymous and opportunistic crowds sold their vote, the system collapsed. That was thousands of years ago; today we bring it again as a novelty, and we face the same blunders again; the consequences of forgetting the past.

Democracy, plainly and simply, does not exist in the natural world. It's inadmissible to subsidize mediocrity. The problem has been, since forever, the manipulation of chaotic masses; and you don't need to resort to violence to achieve it. A very significant point to highlight is that in the regimes that we consider totalitarian and repressive, with a severe control of their citizens, demonstrations of discontent and dissidence occur on a regular basis, even when this entails an exemplary punishment such as imprisonment or death. Do you know how many protests there are against the government system in countries that boast about being free? NONE. Despite misery, hunger, lack of access to health or educational services, and many other hardships, no one protests; buying a good bargain or watching a football game is enough to comfort us. Bread and circus, like the Romans millennia ago. We're the perfect archetype of a society with a null consciousness and a lifeless judgment.

And putting the feet on the ground, to consolidate an effective government regime, apart from being based on Nature and our human condition, an inviolable norm must be instituted: Political power must be, totally and mandatorily, separated from economic power, and even more from religious power. Without these conditions there is not a single possibility of succeeding. It's imperative to establish clear rules that prevent those who head governments from accumulating all authority and wealth. Executive power must never be concentrated in a single person, a triumvirate would be ideal; the councils of elders of the ancient and current indigenous cultures are the best example to follow to have more involved and trustworthy rulers. And it must be composed, precisely, of old people because experience is irreplaceable, no matter how much young people claim to be very capable and come loaded with degrees and diplomas. One of the most insurmountable obstacles that has prevented our evolution is the pride of man in his youth. Each generation aims at creating a "new and better" world. Instead of taking the next step by tapping into the host of wisdom that humanity as a whole has accumulated over millennia, it disdains it, and condemns itself to repeat old mistakes.

In the legislative branch, although decision-making through a general assembly by direct vote is desirable, in today's countries, with so many inhabitants, it is impractical; for this reason, the selection of genuinely committed representatives is paramount. Ultimately, the election of a candidate for any government post must be the result of a voting; but the proper functioning of any electoral system depends on the **quality of its voters.** Not everyone has the right to vote because not everyone has the intellectual capacity to decide what is most convenient for a country according to both internal and external political, social and economic circumstances. People who want to vote must earn the right, by first fulfilling the obligation to prepare to be able to make a thoughtful judgment and not just look out for their interests. As simple as forcing them to take an exam on key topics such as economics, social and health sciences, geography, history, ethics, to evaluate their aptitudes. Whoever passes it earns the right to vote. And the same must be applied to candidates for public office. The creation of a college degree that teaches to be a good ruler is essential; but not the current political or administrative sciences which are a true insult to intelligence. It's necessary to established a career, of some two years, additional to a profession that is at least technical, that is totally focused on government management. Only those who pass it with high grades will be able to aspire to hold a position in the government since it is indispensable that they are well prepared and informed to make decisions. It's necessary to legislate so that the great millionaires, those who receive economic incentives from the state, criminals and ignoramuses are banned from any government decision as an essential mechanism to avert corruption, and to be able to really benefit the entire community. Lobbying, which is nothing more than a vile bribery, must be prohibited and classified for what it is: A perverse crime. A final consideration of capital importance, the salary of government employees must be linked to the income of the lower classes of the social pyramid. This is a decisive tool to try to ensure the vocation of public servants. It is not legal that they want to get an administrative position to enrich themselves with the efforts of the others; plenty of misfortune is to bear the scourge of bureaucracy. The day when the fact of being sit in an office, playing the dumbass, was considered as work, mankind was screwed over forever. In accordance with natural precepts, only the most capable people must rise to leadership positions to make the most convenient decisions and attain true advancement as a society. This also implies that it's indispensable to give a definitive solution to the primary motives for conflict in every human community: The lack of an authentic social consciousness and injustice. If we do not work together for the common good, we all lose out.

Let's examine History again. Given our prejudiced reluctance to achieve real social progress, and our admiration for frivolity and the preeminence of power and wealth as a reflection of our own complexes and frustrations, since antiquity, truly abhorrent beings have been allowed to occupy hegemonic positions, causing hideous calamities. We have a whole series of glorified and triumphant conquerors who were nothing more than despicable murderers who plundered, raped and devastated peoples just to satisfy their greed and their perverted thirst for dominance. Sick guys who, nevertheless, are considered the great heroic personages of history, who must be idolized. Have you heard of Genghis Kahn, Alexander the Great, Julius Caesar and so very many others? That's how disrupted our values are. Here it's imperative to point out the shameful and contemptible role that the armies of the world have played throughout the ages in supporting these disgusting tyrants. Thanks to the servile complicity of so many befuddled patriots, that pack of pigs could spread its noxious influence to all corners of the planet. Today, with the arms industry as a pillar of the economy of the great powers, the advance of military technology and its destructive capacity have reached aberrant degrees. Terrifying weapons that allow to massacre with impunity defenseless women and children from the ignominious safety of an airplane or a ship, hiding behind the mean argument of collateral damage to justify such indescribable suffering. The most inconceivable thing is that, despite such iniquities, these cowards still aim to be regarded as heroes. Long gone are the times of the authentic warriors who, sword in hand, fought in close combats against their peers to prove their true manliness or to defend their ideals.

The natural world has a leisurely cadence that not only allows to understand and ponder, but also to enjoy life at every step. Things mature and happen in due time, and if you try to speed them up because of a banal stubbornness, you're going to spoil them. Yes, patience is a virtue. It's been a long time since we forgot the vital pleasure of contemplation, the act of sitting quietly to admire the landscape, to feel the wind, to listen to the earth. They have instilled in us the notion that in Nature everything is violence, and that in it the law of the jungle governs, where only the strongest one survives. That's how appalling our ignorance is. In the jungle, it is not the strongest one who survives, not even the most intelligent, but the best adapted, the wisest and the most astute one. This we must understand very well. The acceleration in which we live in the Artifiture does not favor reflection. We're engaged in an absurd competition, without having the slightest idea of where we're going, let alone why we're going there; we just run unrestrainedly, like idiots. In our mad eagerness to beat time, to force things, we have disguised imbecility as efficiency, and mediocrity as modernism. We have even arbitrarily modified the natural time to get the most out of it. You already know, our twisted concept that time is money. Our "avant-garde" mentality is summarized in a very in vogue saying, originated from advertising, and that presumably should motivate even the most apathetic: Just do it! Nothing is further from reality. To carry out a project you must first know it, then evaluate it, get prepared and, finally, do it. Precipitation has led us to countless failures and very regrettable mistakes. But if it becomes fashionable, everyone imitates it. Never the slightest doubt arises that these silly values may be wrong. We cannot give higher priority to the trivial role assigned to us in a decadent society, which is destructing itself, than to that which we have in Nature and for which we have been endowed with the necessary faculties. The ultimate goal is to get a vision of your own of the world, grounded in reality, in order to escape manipulation and its deceitful reasonings. Do the words health, family, freedom still mean something to you? We claim to be very self-sufficient and with the ability to innovate the world and adjust it to our whims and desires. We forget that we've been on earth for thousands of years and, in essence, nothing has changed; so much distorted science and technology are not enough, the beast remains in us. Don't you believe it? As simple as removing electricity, like when a storm or a hurricane hit. With that simple contingency, not only the XXI century is finished, but even the XX. This is how fragile and insignificant the wondrous world we have built is. We're a serious disease for the planet. We have caused it a severe ecological imbalance that threatens the lives of all beings that inhabit it, including, irrationally, ours. Like the plague, which, on annihilating its victim, it kills itself.

CHAPTER VIII

THE HORRIFYING ERRORS!

The Farewell Verity

In the true world we must learn to live, PERIOD! There are two ways to do it: the easy way, using your intelligence, or the hard way, letting life teach you by force of real blows. It's up to you. The crucial point of this learning lies, simply, in becoming aware that we're inescapably obliged to **make the minimum possible errors** in our passage on earth. The fewer mistakes, the less time we will waste and the further we'll go, hopefully we'll even reach the human level. For those who want to avoid them, these are very easy to identify. The path is very clear, diaphanous, there is no reason to get confused or go astray. There is no mystery. Only to the unwary who lets himself to be manipulated by advertising, things will get complicated since it's going to create trivial, false needs, and he will have to pay the consequences. The first thing is to get rid of so many foreign prejudices and complexes, the fruits of domestication. The final destiny of human life is to be part of the harmony of Cosmos; to be useful! Therein lie all the happiness and the satisfaction of the accomplished duty that give meaning to our existence. The key is in not losing focus on the fundamental values, although your interests change naturally as age makes you mature; nothing to worry about. So, let us analyze those so horrific errors:

1.- ***To move away from Nature.*** – It is the most serious; fatal to the soul. Nature is our very essence; only in it the Human Being succeeds in expressing himself and fully develop his capabilities. It's the sole really valid and authentic thing. Its wisdom is irreplaceable. Nothing substitutes the experience of entering into communion with the Universe. Step out into the countryside; listen to the silence! Let yourself be wrapped by the simplicity of life. Do not cram your space with material things; it's not true that you need them to be happy.

2.- ***To neglect Health.*** – There is no more precious treasure; neither gold nor money, NOTHING is worth more. With it you'll be free, you'll have the energy to carry out projects, to dream and to enjoy life to the fullest. But, beware! In our materialistic civilization it is totally devalued; it's the last thing we take into account. They want to deceive us with mirages, vain promises of fictitious liberties: Technology, drugs, excesses, noise and many other noxious trivial matters. Don't you fall into the trap.

3.- ***To waste time.*** – Life is a sigh. It's essential to know yourself, and, as soon as possible, become aware of reality, as an invariable parameter to guide our conduct. To set goals and deadlines at the earliest opportunity. Study, preparation, reflection, are paramount. The more intellectual and spiritual weapons you have, the higher the probability of reaching the objective. It's unacceptable that after the age of twenty-four, namely one third of the lifespan that current expectations allow, an individual has no notion yet of what he's going to do in life. And for someone who has less time left to live than what he has already lived, to be still in limbo is a resounding failure; a chilling proof of his mediocrity and stupidity.

4.- ***To try to deny Reality.*** – The laws of Nature are immovable. We are not all equal! We must have the courage to accept our limitations, and be the best within the range of our own abilities. Do not claim to be who you are not or to obtain what you do not deserve. Authenticity is one of the most invaluable virtues. To reach the maturity of not needing rewards for committing to our convictions is the sole thing that leads us to happiness.

5.- *To forget that obligations come first and then rights.* – The road is hard; constant effort, inevitable; privileges are only earned by fulfilling duties. Things that are really worthwhile are very few and take hard work to obtain. Do not expect magic, easy or immediate solutions. Perseverance, discipline, commitment, are indispensable; there is no way to put them aside. And all this takes time. Therefore, the main point is to understand that not only reaching the goal is important, but also enjoying the journey.

6.- *To procreate children before reaching emotional and financial stability.* – First of all, it's essential not to have children until after four years of cohabitation with your couple, to give an opportunity for passion to subside, and for reason to enter to evaluate what the true probabilities are that the relationship will last for a long time. So that children do not grow up without one of the parents! To beget a child solely because you are incapable of finding another way to fill your spiritual void, or in order to conform with absurd social patterns, is one of the most monumental errors, and reveals a maximum degree of selfishness and wickedness. And not only because you're going to limit your own possibilities for personal development, sinking into anxiety and frustration, but because you're going to condemn your offspring to scarcity and adversities, denying them the opportunity to have a free and full life. So much evilness is unforgivable!

7.- *Not having the fortitude to forge your own destiny.* – It's essential to avoid getting involved with vulgar, idiotic or perverse people. There are heaps of them. They wander senselessly and never succeed in reaching happiness; they will only lead you to a vacuous and futile existence, to failure as a Human Being. It's stupid to seek recognition from others. Go your own path. Don't you get carried away by ideologies, of any kind: Religious, economic, political, social. They were concocted by malevolent and unscrupulous guys, parasites who only want to take advantage of the masses. Fashion and the obsessive pursuit of physical beauty are the grossest and most humiliating forms of manipulation, especially if one is mentally and spiritually hollow and deformed. The majority will always be servile, submissive, pusillanimous; mediocre people willing to debase themselves, to grovel to gain favors, for not to fight. To be a part of it is the greatest shame imaginable. If you think like them, you'll end up being like them. ***The elusive and precious freedom is one of the supreme desires to which the true Human Being aspires.*** But freedom is born in individuality, in solitude. There is a very simple rule that is infallible: Do the opposite of what the herd does. If they say you have to try drugs, don't do it; if they say you have to watch football, don't do it; if they say you have to get into technology, don't do it. It's not true that it's indispensable, vital; no matter how much the merchants' ambition harps on about it.

And up to here I get. I'm already tired of writing so much bullshit. And, indeed, there is not that much to say. The really essential things in life are extraordinarily few. We've already seen that the fingers of one hand suffice to count them: Nature, Health, Time, Freedom, and Love, as the adhesive that holds it all together. The rest is garbage; expendable, superfluous banalities. Not all that glitters is gold. Negative experiences maim the mind and the soul. The force of reality must make us question our beliefs and behaviors. Before rejecting the ideas, presented, I invite you to reflect for a moment on what gets you upset about them: To realize your mediocrity? Your inability to face reality? To situate your littleness in the universal context? To comprehend the deception that we're not children of god, but just one more of the insignificant beings that inhabit the planet? What is it that terrifies you the most? A wise man already said it a very long time ago: ***Reality does not need to prove that it exists. When we forget it, it contents itself with doing harm.*** It's imperative to understand that there are no valid arguments to refute reality. And the best of all is that in it we can dare to dream and be free. This must be a new dawn, a rectification of the course towards a true evolution to reach the human condition, and to fully incorporate ourselves into the everlasting cycle of this, our Wondrous Universe.

Never forget it: God, we can send him to fuck his mother. To Nature, NO!